Ribbons

LAURENCE YEP

G. P. PUTNAM'S SONS
NEW YORK

G. P. Putnam's Sons, a division of The Putnam & Grosset Group,

200 Madison Avenue, New York, NY 10016.

G. P. Putnam's Sons, Reg. U.S. Pat. & Tm. Off.

Published simultaneously in Canada. Printed in the United States of America

Book design by Donna Mark. Text set in Goudy Old Style.

A portion of this book was originally published by

Pleasant Company Publications in *American Girl* magazine.

Library of Congress Cataloging-in-Publication Data

Yep, Laurence. Ribbons / Laurence Yep.   p. cm.

Summary: Robin, a promising young ballet student, cannot afford to continue

lessons when her Chinese grandmother emigrates from Hong Kong, creating

jealousy and conflict among the entire family.

[1. Chinese Americans—Fiction. 2. Grandmothers—Fiction. 3. Ballet

dancing—Fiction. 4. Chinese—United States—Fiction. 5. Family life—Fiction.]

I. Title. PZ7.Y44Ri 1996   [Fic]—dc20   95-33488   CIP   AC

ISBN 0-399-22906-X

1 3 5 7 9 10 8 6 4 2

First Impression

To Emilya, Jo, Christen and Lucy,
Mermaids all.

• CONTENTS •

Ribbons

The Recital

This year everything went wrong with our shortened *Nutcracker*. As soon as the mice began battling the soldiers beneath the Christmas tree, a fat little girl, dressed as a soldier, got carried away and whacked a boy, dressed as a mouse, on the head with her sword. Because of the thick padding, she hurt his pride more than his head, but he began to cry anyway.

As soon as they heard the blubbering, the rest of the beginners' class paused onstage to see what the matter was. And then they just milled about, the entire class of soldiers and mice having forgotten the choreography.

There's quite a difference between practice and performance. Suddenly the auditorium seems as deep and black as a cavern. And the spotlights shine in your eyes so brightly that it's painful. When those merciless lights hit you for the first time, it's like being splashed with a magical brew that drives every thought out of your head—even your own name.

And if that isn't scary enough, there is an audience out there. It lurks within the darkness beyond the lights like some huge multiheaded beast, coughing, breathing, rattling its programs, and waiting for the slightest mistake. So I sympathized.

The little girls had even put on a little eyeliner for the first time to emphasize their eyes for the stage—even though they were dressed as soldiers. I singled out the nearest and hissed, "Cecily."

When Cecily remained as frozen as a military statue, I tried again—willing her to look at me: "Cecily."

This time her head jerked toward where I stood in the wings. "Like this, remember?" And I did a couple of the steps.

However, the eyes remained dazed, as if she did not see me at all. I suppose it's how a deer's eyes look when it sees the headlights of a truck rushing toward it. From the beast beyond the blackness, I heard a titter.

"It starts this way." I repeated the steps again.

To my relief, I saw her head jerk up and down like a marionette's, almost losing her helmet until she balanced it with one hand. Facing the audience again, she began the dance—though she was now several bars behind the music. The girls next to her saw her and like little robots started to copy her.

The trouble was that Cecily went blank after the steps I had shown her. However, being a trouper, she tried to wing it by bouncing around. In no time, the mice and soldiers were improvising the battle. One of them stumbled into the wings on the other side, almost knocking over the school's old stereo. As it was, Stokowski's recording would never be the same.

Everyone—from beginners to advanced students—froze again in horror as the record began to skip. Cecily began to cry, and her tears made the eyeliner run in black stripes down her face.

"Eveline," I whispered urgently.

Eveline was the best dancer in the advanced class, but she was just standing with a hand to her cheek, horrified at the disaster.

At seventeen, she was six years older than me, but I thought I'd better take things in hand. Forcing myself to smile, I swiped bits of the choreography from *Swan Lake*, which we had been practicing in the lower advanced class, and danced across the stage in my Morning Butterfly costume, with leaps that were probably more energetic than graceful. Somehow I made it through the combatants to the other wing. Going to the stereo, I elbowed it.

The music resumed its triumphal progress as the needle skipped ahead. To its rhythm, I glided back on stage, where they were still all standing like mannequins. "Keep going," I whispered to them.

I grabbed the nearest soldier and steered her toward where she should be for this part of the music. And then, trying to smile all the time, I started to snag other soldiers and mice and desperately started to rearrange them.

My friend Amy got the idea and improvised some steps as a Dresden Doll to come onstage. When she nodded her head to Leah Brown, the head Snow Flake, Leah followed her. Thomas, who was Mother Goose, took charge of the beginners who doubled as his children in the second act.

Though I was in the lower advanced class and Amy, Leah, and Thomas were in the upper intermediate class, we all had been beginners together and had served our time as soldiers and mice. So we knew the simple steps.

It wasn't long before the recital resumed. I looked for Madame Oblamov, our teacher. I was sure she'd had a heart attack, but I couldn't see beyond the foot of the stage because the lights were shining in my eyes. I could not see even my family, though I had marked seats for them in the front row.

After we had gotten the beginners in sync with the music again, my friends and I exited. Thomas was doing his best not to laugh, and Amy and Leah had their hands over their mouths.

Eveline was sitting on a foldout chair. She had to lean forward at an extreme angle because of her fairy wings. "I don't see what's so funny," she glowered, quite un-fairylike.

There was applause for the beginners, but, except for their parents, it was coolly polite. However, the young ones were too excited to notice. I'd been like them once. Applause was applause. All that practice, all that boredom, all that sweat—suddenly they all become worthwhile.

As soldiers and mice streamed past, Leah led her snow flakes onstage. Leah was the only intermediate: the others were all beginners, dressed for the first time in sequins and crinoline. She was part dancer and part drill instructor onstage during the journey of Clara and the Prince to the Land of the Sweets. (And we had no sleighs like they have in the big productions. Poor Clara and the Prince had to hoof it).

During the short intermission, I was kept busy helping the mice and soldiers out of their costumes and into costumes as angels, gumdrops, flowers, and Mother Goose's children.

Once Clara and the Prince had arrived, at the opening of the second act, the celebrating began. My stomach started to do flip-flops as my own cue drew near.

Soon it would be time for the Morning Butterfly to stumble across the stage. I tried to breathe slowly and deeply; but then it was my turn to panic because suddenly I couldn't remember the steps.

From the opposite wing, Amy and Leah frantically

began to wave for me to go on. My feet seemed glued to the spot. Months and months of hard work for a few minutes of glory in the spotlight, and I was going to fall and keep falling. Ballerinas were like figure skaters that way. I wasn't about to embarrass myself in front of my friends and family by going out there.

"Go on," Thomas hissed, and he shoved me from behind.

I staggered out onto the stage. Beyond the planks of the stage, there seemed to be nothing but a black vacuum. And the spotlights shone on me like bright, white-hot stars. For a moment, I felt as if one misstep would plunge me into the emptiness, falling forever.

But after long weeks of rehearsal, the music had soaked into my very flesh. As I heard the familiar notes, my body remembered for me. My arms began to move gently, instinctively, to the music, and my torso started to sway. But I was stiff at first. I was sure somewhere in the darkness, Madame must be wincing.

The lights were almost blinding as I moved nearer to the foot of the stage. I could see the other dancers in their poses, faces garish with makeup. Beyond the lights, I could hear the audience—still coughing and wriggling and flapping their programs. What made me think I could ever please that multiheaded creature that was the audience?

And then I heard a small pair of hands begin to clap. I knew that had to be Ian. At five, he could be clapping for me or, more likely, because he hoped the ballet was already over. A moment later a double pair of larger hands joined in—which had to be my parents. Their applause echoed against the low ceiling of the auditorium. It sounded almost tinny, in fact, but it gave me the courage to go on.

Long neck and long legs gave a natural line to my body. Raising my arm, I began a running step and launched into a grand jeté.

Leaping was my strong point. Even when I was small, I could hop like a rabbit long after my friends had dropped to the ground in exhaustion. Though I felt stiff when I sprang from the floor, my body started to relax with the familiar motion, and I extended one leg forward. For a moment, I felt as if I were suspended in air, and then I landed in an arabesque. As I stood there for a moment, I heard applause again—this time genuine. I had tamed that multiheaded creature.

I began to really dance then. It was just me and the music now. And I forgot about the audience or even to be afraid.

Suddenly I no longer felt like I was in a simple school production. Instead, I was in a real ballet company. The boxlike auditorium was a real theater. And I was one of a long line of ballerinas who had danced the butterfly. As the boards creaked beneath me, I could feel their ghosts dancing beside me.

Time itself seemed to stop then, and all there was

was my body and the music. In the back of my mind, there was a voice telling me what I was going to have to do next and perhaps some step to be careful on because I had muffed it in practice. It was a voice that only long hours of practice could create. But most of me simply enjoyed feeling my body move through the air as if it were floating.

I wished the joy could last forever and ever, but eventually it had to end. And then I just stood there, dazed, as the last note of music faded from the speakers.

The silence was as sharp as a knife. Had the audience stayed? Did they like me? And then the applause crashed around me like the waves of an ocean. And the audience's approval was as bright and hot as the lights that bathed me. There was nothing like dance when everything went right—and nothing quite like it when everything went wrong. But at the moment, all was right with the world. I could have stood there forever, but the needle kept on its inexorable march, and the next dancers swept out.

Later, after the finale, as we all stepped onto the stage, I looked for my friend Amy. Over the head of a Russian Cossack, I found her. Though her thick mask of makeup made her look like a stranger, she smiled at me. Beyond her, Leah, the head Snow Flake, gave me a thumbs-up. On my other side, Thomas winked.

It never fails. No matter how often we rehearse the

curtain calls, there are always a couple of beginners who get so excited that they forget. When the rest of us retreated, they were supposed to stay in front and drop a curtsy. (As Thomas would say, " 'Cute' must have its time in the spotlight, after all.") Same as always, several of them fell back with us. Catching themselves, they tried to bounce forward precisely when the rest of the beginners were moving back. They just stood there confused as the intermediates moved through the ranks of the beginners and blundered into them.

"Once more, dear friends, into the breach," Thomas whispered in his high-pitched Julia Child voice. Thomas could do everything. Dancer. Mime. Comic. Actor. Puppeteer. I had no doubts that Thomas would become a big star one day.

"Give us a hand, Robin," Leah whispered.

So I moved forward with the intermediate class instead of the advanced one. We smoothly disentangled the beginners and guided them downstage with gentle shoves. Then we bounded to the foot of the stage and took our curtsies and bows.

"Now," Thomas said then. I don't know how or when he had worked it out with the others, but they pulled back, leaving me in front. I would have retreated with them, but Thomas put a hand to my back to keep me there. "You saved us from disaster, Robin."

Feeling as dumb as a beginner, I stood there a moment. I felt a mixture of joy and embarrassment as the applause swelled in volume. And as I stared at the bright lights, I knew that I wanted to hold on to this feeling for the rest of my life.

Then the rest of the advanced class stepped up around me, and I was surrounded by "cattle," as Thomas called the other classes. Though Eveline and the other lead dancers got their share of applause, it wasn't as heartfelt as mine had been.

Giggles mixed with excited voices as we flowed offstage. I found Madame Oblamov by the stereo, mourning the large old vinyl record. "What is *Swan Lake* without Stokowski conducting it?"

I knew from Madame's sister, who played the piano during classes, that it had taken all she could do to get Madame to switch to vinyl from 78's.

I could see the jagged scratch on the old record Madame held between her fingertips. "Can't you can buy another one?"

Madame's shrugs were massive and eloquent. "Where? Nowadays it is all teeny seabees."

It took me a moment to realize she was referring to CD's. "Maybe we can find another one at a used-record store."

Madame Oblamov tucked the record under her arm. She was a large woman. It had been many years since she had posed as a slim dancer for the photos that hung on her wall. She had danced with the Leningrad Ballet until she defected in Copenhagen. (Amy and Leah were convinced that the story was as exciting and thrilling as a spy movie.) Madame's framed newspaper articles of her various triumphs were in five languages. Like her photos, though, they were fading to a pale brown color like rectangles of leather.

She perked up with the first glimmerings of hope. "There are such things?"

"Shall I get the telephone book?" I offered. I was already starting for her office when she stopped me.

Madame grew even sadder. "What a treasure! How I shall miss you." Looking as if she were going to cry, Madame gathered me up in her hamlike arms and crushed me against the corsage on her white silk blouse.

Just as suddenly, she released me, as if holding me only deepened her sorrow. Wanting a distraction, she turned to greet my parents before her words could finish registering in my brain: *Miss me?*

Suddenly I felt as if I just stepped off the stage and plunged into that fearful darkness.

The Debt

Mom and Dad had my brother, Ian, in tow as they came up the steps to the stage. Ian was still clutching the end of a roll of Lifesavers that had kept him quiet during the recital.

"Good evening, Madame," Mom said politely. She spoke with a trace of a British accent that she had picked up as a girl in the Hong Kong schools.

"Quite a triumph," Dad said, hugging me proudly. "You look so pretty in blue, hon."

I returned his hug and whispered, "Pink, Dad. My costume's pink." Dad's color blind.

"You are such a joker." Madame, who liked to flirt with the fathers, took a chunk of Dad's cheek and pinched it. "It would have been a disaster without Robin."

Grimacing, Dad retreated beyond Madame's reach. "I often feel that way myself."

"But now to important matters. Your daughter," Madame announced in her stately fashion, "has talent. Won't you change your mind?"

Mom and Dad stood embarrassed. "We've already discussed the reasons," Mom said finally.

"The other students here just want to wear pretty costumes. But your daughter has real promise." Madame was too dignified to plead openly, but her eyes spoke for her. "I saw it in Robin's first recital when she was so small. A beginner herself! All the others froze, but she went right on. And I said to myself, 'There is a dancer!'"

Dad proudly hefted up his camcorder—it looked big enough to be a starship cannon—and looked through the viewfinder for a good shot. "She is good, isn't she?"

Mom shook her head. "We just can't handle lessons right now."

Madame heaved a great sigh. "Then let Robin return to me soon."

"Madame, you're not sending me away," I said in distress.

Madame caressed my cheek regretfully. "I wish I could afford to give scholarships, because if I could, you would be the first. You have so much promise. But it is so expensive to run a school."

I caught Madame's hand, refusing to let go. "But Madame—"

She pursed her lips together to make a shushing sound. "In the meantime, keep practicing And I will pray for the day when you return to me." She paused as she tried to get her voice back. In the corners of her eyes, I thought I saw tears.

"Now excuse me. I must find Stokowski." She tore her hand from mine and turned toward her office. After all these years, Madame could still move gracefully across the floor, though her full figure now made her look like a stately galleon under sail. As she disappeared inside, I thought I saw her wipe at her eyes.

Hoping against hope, I turned to Dad. "What does Madame mean?"

"Ian has something for you," Dad said. With one hand, he kept the camcorder up to his eye, and with his other, he nudged my little brother.

As the camcorder began to roll, a scowling Ian stepped forward and presented me with a single rose. "Here."

Out of sight of the lens, Dad poked my brother again. "What do you have to say first?"

With a grimace, Ian closed his eyes and recited like a parrot: "In the future, you'll get lots of big bouquets. So . . . so . . ." His face screwed up anxiously as he sought to remember his speech. Dad stopped taping long enough to lean over and whisper in his ear. "Oh, yeah," Ian said with a nod. "So-let-this-rose-be-the-first-of-many," he rattled off rapidly, as if he were afraid he might forget if he took his time.

I was still in a state of shock, but I managed to thank him. Laying it on the floor, I sat on a nearby folding chair while I unwound the ribbons of my ballet shoes. At eleven I was tall for my age, so Madame had let me wear pointe shoes. I had been so proud the first time I wound the ribbons around my ankles.

Now, though, I just felt lost as I held them in my hands. The lights started going out in the auditorium, and Madame's sister got ready to close up the school. Suddenly my magical costume became just sequins and crinoline again.

"Come on, honey." Lowering the camcorder, Dad dangled my sneakers before me. They looked so big and ugly and clumsy in comparison to my toe shoes that I almost hated to put them on.

Cradling my pointe shoes on my lap, I forced my feet into the other pair. They felt all hot and clunky, and when I took the first couple of steps in them, I felt as if I now had hooves.

I picked up the satin bag decorated with stars. Leah and Amy had given that to me when Madame had declared I was big enough to wear toe shoes—the first in the group. I stowed the shoes carefully inside and pulled the drawstring shut.

Leah was small for her age, so she still wore the regular ballet slippers. But Amy was almost my height—though thinner—so it was only a matter of time before she joined me on pointe.

Dad helped me disengage my butterfly wings and

draped my coat over my costume. Then my parents led me out of the school. "What was Madame talking about, Dad?" I asked again.

Tucking my wings under the same arm that held the camcorder, Dad grabbed my shoulder and steered me outside onto the sidewalk. "Better say good-bye to your friends."

Outside was a swirl of students and their families making their farewells for the holidays, and the street was clogged with triple-parked cars.

Studiously trying to ignore her mother, who was videotaping her, Leah chatted with Amy's mother and the rest of Amy's big Chinese family. As usual, though, Thomas had no one. His family never came to the recitals, and the one time I had asked he had simply smirked. "You wouldn't want them drooling on people," he had said. He stood there now with a raincoat over his costume. He had taken off Mother Goose's hooped skirt and had it slung over his shoulder like a collapsed plaid beehive, but his frilly pantaloons protruded from beneath his raincoat.

He was busy making plans to go the Video Café for ice cream with some of the other students. All of them were still energized from the performance, so they were almost bouncing up and down on the balls of their feet. Some had not bothered to put on coats over their costumes. We all probably looked like escapees from a flying saucer.

Excusing myself from my family, I went over to them. When Amy turned around, I saw that she hadn't wiped off her makeup yet. Up close and in the light from the streetlamps, it seemed very garish now that the magic of the performance had ended. I always felt a little sad after a show was done, and I felt even worse now because of Madame's dismissal.

"Oh, there you are, Robin," Amy said. "Do you want to go for ice cream?"

I was usually hungry after a performance, and I hadn't eaten any sweets this week in anticipation of having a dessert with my dancemates. However, the dreadful news had killed my appetite. I shook my head, still in a daze. "Madame said something about my leaving the school."

Leah clutched at the neck of her coat, which she had thrown on over her costume. "What? You're not going to break up the gang . . . ," she protested.

Thomas improvised a fist puppet, holding his knuckles parallel to the sidewalk and moving his thumb like a lower lip. His own lips barely moved as he said, "You're going to stay, of course."

"They can't do this to you. You're her star pupil. And how will Madame remember where she puts things? You're the one who tells her." Thomas put his hand under his chin and adopted his best bedside manner. "You're delirious. This definitely calls for two doses of mint chocolate chip."

My parents were standing apart with Ian. "No, I have to talk this over with my folks."

"I'll call you tomorrow," Amy promised.

Waving good-bye to the others, I rejoined my folks. "Now, will you explain what Madame meant?"

"Not here, Robin, darling," Mom said. "Let's not have a scene."

Poor Ian made the mistake of making a face. "You smell all sweaty."

I took out my frustrations by leaning over and rubbing my cheek against his in mock affection. "You're no rose yourself." When I straightened up, I was satisfied to see that I had left a sizable smear of rouge upon my little brother's cheek. With a little luck, some of his friends would see him.

Still unaware of the greasepaint, Ian stiffened. "I am too a rose." He hesitated. "I think," he added—as if he were assaulted by sudden doubts about whether that was a compliment or an insult.

We lived in the Richmond district, which is a sandy patch in the northwest corner of San Francisco. When the fog drifted in from the ocean, it halted at a line of hills that ran down the center of San Francisco. The old cemeteries had been there for years, and visitors could leave flowers and stare westward over the foggy dunes toward the gray ocean. The constant ocean wind sent slender snakes of sand wriggling up and down the dunes.

After World War Two, though, a lot of returning soldiers had wanted to live in San Francisco, and identical boxlike houses sprang up like mushrooms. But back then it was no more than a thin skin of asphalt and cement stretched over great sand dunes. Sometimes on nights like this, I thought the sand snakes must resent having all the heavy houses on top of them. And if I put my ear to the sidewalk, I would hear them prowling beneath the cement layer.

Some of my schoolmates from the sunnier, ritzier parts of San Francisco found Richmond dreary and called the buildings here "ticky-tacky boxes." But I wouldn't have traded it for anything. Dad liked to say Richmond was like some foggy spot on the ancient Silk Road, where cultures met.

When Dad was a boy, the neighborhood had been mainly Russian. And then when they changed the immigration quotas and enacted the fair housing laws, a lot of Chinese had moved in. In fact, people started to call our area the "New Chinatown." However, now that the Soviet Union had broken up, a lot of Russians were again flooding into the neighborhood.

It makes for a fun mixture now. There are Russian bakeries next to Chinese delicatessens. You can buy Russian books and listen to Chinese music. And the corner grocery stores are owned by Arabs. Sometimes I felt like I didn't have to go away to see the world, because the world came to see me.

As we walked toward our flat, I had so much energy from the recital that I would have danced anyway And my anxieties only added fuel to my tank.

When I was four, I saw a ballet on television. The ballerinas seemed so beautiful and elegant as they moved on pointe. I wanted to belong to their lovely world. Everywhere I went, I used to pretend I was one of those graceful creatures, until Mom would groan and beg me to walk regularly in the supermarket.

As soon as I was old enough, I got Mom to enroll me at a ballet school in the neighborhood. Mom had picked it because it was convenient; she thought ballet was just a phase I was going through. She couldn't have known that the elderly Russian lady was a famous teacher.

Most of the other little girls just wanted an excuse to bounce around in a pretty costume. I was one of the few who took the class seriously. Madame quickly discovered that I could turn out my legs almost like an adult ballerina. It was some freak of nature, like being double jointed, but I could turn my legs in their hip joints so that my feet could form a straight line. It took most dancers years of work to get their legs to do that. I was so proud when Madame had told me.

As we stopped at a traffic light, Ian brought me out of my reveries. "Did you hear me clap, Robin?"

He reminded me that just when I began to think Ian was the worst brat in the world, he would do things like that. "I certainly did. Thank you."

"The others were just sitting there." He frowned and glanced up at me. "I thought you looked so pretty."

"You do?" I asked in surprise.

"For a girl." As he started to scratch his cheek, he suddenly became suspicious. Lifting his hand away, he examined his fingertips under the dim light of the streetlamp.

I'd take a compliment where I could get it. I got a Kleenex from my coat pocket and I wiped the makeup from his face. "Want me to show you how to pirouette?"

"I already know how." He spun around on one ankle. By the time, the light had changed to green again, he was pretty wobbly.

"Come on, handsome." I held out my hand.

When he took mine, I could feel how sticky his palm was from all the Lifesavers that Mom and Dad fed him to keep quiet during the show.

I held on to it anyway as we crossed at the light. And I was still at it when we reached home. We lived in a flat that formed the third story of the building, with another flat below us. Like a lot of houses and flats in Richmond, the ground floor was a two-car garage.

After we had put Ian to bed, my parents sat down with me around the kitchen table. "You know we've been working for years to get your grandmother over," Mom said.

It had been the sole ambition of my mother and her

brothers to bring their mother from Hong Kong to San Francisco. In fact, the last few months that was all Mom talked about, but I confined myself to a cautious "Yes."

"We're so close now," Dad tried to explain, "but we have to save every cent for that."

Mom tried to make me feel guilty. "You don't want her in Hong Kong when the Communists take over, do you?" In a few years the British were scheduled to return their colony to China.

Mom looked hurt. "It's taken five years of phone calls to coax her to leave. I don't want to let her change her mind."

I had never met my grandmother, but Dad had. When he had married Mom, they went back to Hong Kong on their honeymoon. From little things he said, I don't think she had taken to the idea of a Caucasian son-in-law.

"No," Dad sighed. "She's sure to say something that will get her shot."

"Gil!"

"Just kidding." Dad hastily grabbed the camcorder and raised it now like a shield.

"But why do I have to end my lessons with Madame?" I pleaded.

Mom sucked in her breath through her teeth. "You're eleven. That's old enough to understand. You don't hear Ian complaining."

They might as well have told me that they wanted me to cut off my foot. Life without lessons . . . without Madame . . . It wasn't even what I would call living. "What will happen to my skills?"

Dad fiddled with the camcorder in front of him. A documentary maker, he was always happier with his equipment. "It's just for a while," Dad said soothingly. "In the meantime, you can practice at home."

"But I'll get behind everyone," I argued.

Mom sighed wearily. "Let me get the calculator." She took it from a cabinet drawer where she kept the household accounts and immediately began to work out the figures. "Tuition, leotards, shoes . . ."

As she rattled off items, the numbers climbed until it was more than a thousand dollars.

Dad finally arched an eyebrow questioningly at Mom. "Well?"

Mom punched some more figures into her calculator. Then she bit her lip and shook her head. "It costs so much to get her out. There's the lawyers, the paperwork—lots of things."

Dad ran a hand through his brown hair and tilted back his chair. "Maybe we can cut a few more corners."

"We're already down to the bone." Mom passed the calculator over to him. "Anyway, perhaps it's a blessing in disguise. Robin can move on to other activities after school."

I made do with old clothes, and I didn't expect Nintendos at Christmas. When my friends wanted to go to movies, I said I had to study. I knew I wasn't supposed to ask for things that cost money. And Ian and I were already resigned to only one present each this Christmas.

But all my life I had wanted to be a ballerina. "Can't we find a way?"

Mom glanced at me in disappointment. "Everything is just costing so much more. Even the tea money." Tea money was a polite name for the bribes she had to pay to Chinese officials.

Dad studied the calculator tape a moment longer. "You've got two brothers. I don't see why they can't help."

"They would if they could, but they have expenses," Mom defended them. "Georgie's just getting his electronic store off the ground, and Eddy's bought that house."

Dad put on his bulldog expression. "Well, we have expenses too."

Mom eyed Dad warningly. "You knew when you married me, Gil, that I came as a package with my whole family."

Dad was the first to give in. With a sigh, he ran a hand through his hair. "I just didn't realize how big a package."

I was desperate enough to use every weapon. "Well,

maybe we could try Nana." Nana was my other grandmother, Dad's mother.

"Yes," Dad began. "Why not—"

Mom glared at him. "Because she thinks she can
buy everyone."

Nana often seemed to be a sore point between Dad
and Mom whenever her name came up, but they never
explained why. "What do you mean?" I tried to ask.

Dad gave me the usual answer whenever I tried to
probe deeper: "Never mind."

I sighed in frustration. "You're a lawyer, Mom.
How can we be so poor? I have friends whose parents
are lawyers, and they're all rich."

Mom pressed her lips into a tight smile. "Not when
you're a public interest lawyer."

I turned to Dad. "Why can't you do some commer-
cial work for television, Dad?"

Dad gave me the same smile as Mom had. "Even assuming I'd be willing to stoop so low, it's not that easy
to get those gigs."

Mom cleared her throat. "She has a point, Gil.
When was the last time you shot any film for your
documentary?"

Dad narrowed his eyes, but he fought to keep his
voice even. "Film costs money, and I don't have any
money."

"And you haven't been able to raise money for your
film in months," Mom said.

"Why not quit the *pro bono* cases?" Dad shot back. *Pro bono* meant they were for the public good and were done for free.

Neither one of them was willing to give up their high-minded but impoverished ways. So instead Mom appealed directly to me. "You understand, don't you, Robin, darling? We owe everything to Grandmother."

A widow, she had brought her family to Hong Kong when the Communists had taken over China. It was impossible to argue with the Debt. It was the ultimate trump card.

"I know," I said in a small voice.

"And," Mom added, "I'd be very disappointed if you spoke to anyone about the sacrifices we're making. I don't want her finding out and feeling bad. So you can't even tell her."

What could I do faced with the Debt? "I won't," I promised.

Dad turned to me and shrugged apologetically. "What about afterward?" he asked Mom.

Mom clicked off the calculator. "We'll see."

THREE

Christmas Cheer

Since Madame had closed down the school for the holidays, I had a taste of what my life would be like; and I hated it. As boring and repetitive as the ballet classes could be, they gave me an outlet for my usual energy. Without the classes, I got even more fidgety than Ian—drumming my fingers or waggling my leg or tapping my foot until I drove the rest of my family crazy.

So I called up Amy to see how she was doing. In the background, I could hear her brothers and sisters yelling at one another. Even though it sounded like World War Three, her voice was as chirpy as ever. "Are you getting as antsy as me?"

"Yeah, you too?" I asked. "I feel all guilty—like my muscles are turning to Jell-O."

"One day off and I already feel sloppy and flabby." Amy did her best to imitate Madame, though Madame had a deep voice and Amy's was high. " 'Dancers who don't practice will know it the first time they try to dance.' "

I finished the quote we had both heard so often from Madame. " 'And the next time they miss a practice, everyone else will know it.' " Madame always seemed to sense when we were getting bored or discouraged.

"How about going over to Leah's for practice?" she suggested. "Thomas and I are going there at two." Leah had the luxuries of wooden floors and no neighbors to complain about the thumping of her feet. About ten minutes before two, I walked the few blocks to Leah's house.

Mrs. Brown was a doctor. She had divorced Leah's father long ago and had bought their house. As sweet and kind as Mrs. Brown was, she could be as tough as leather. Leah's mother had been one of the first African-Americans to move onto the block, and she had managed to outlast the cold shoulders and hostile stares. And Leah could be just as tough as her mother.

Their house was a cute pink little box with a garage on the ground floor and an iron gate across the bottom of the stairs that led up to their door on the second floor. Cacti in pots decorated the steps. The joke was that cacti were the only plants that could survive Leah and her mother, who managed to kill most houseplants.

Thomas was already there, his white gangly frame and limbs splayed across an easy chair. He was so busy eating a dish of ice cream that he just waved his spoon at me. "Want some ice cream?" Leah asked.

"You bet," Amy said, and flopped down into the nearest chair.

The sight of Thomas's cool, sweet ice cream made my stomach rumble, but I got control of it quick. I only allowed myself one sweet a week. "None for me," I said.

"You and I can watch," Leah said as she headed for the kitchen. Leah didn't allow herself sugar at all—or much food in general. Mrs. Brown complained that Leah just lived off cooking aromas. I was sure that at the celebration the other night she had satisfied herself with a spoonful of Thomas's ice cream.

The constant dieting, though, seemed to put pouches under her eyes, which gave her a perpetually nervous look. She stared at the ice cream wistfully as she handed it to Amy. "If I didn't have my father's big bones, I could eat like Thomas."

I was a little annoyed with Thomas and Amy, who never seemed to put on any weight. "You don't have big bones," I said to Leah. "But even if you did, you'd never be a pig like Thomas."

Thomas set the bowl down on a small side table, the spoon clinking musically against the porcelain side. "I'll have you know that I am helping Leah celebrate."

"Celebrate?" I asked.

"Come and see." Leah took my hand and started to pull me toward the stairs leading to the third floor. Thomas followed, licking some melted chocolate ice cream from his thumb.

Leah stopped at the door that led to the guest bedroom. "Voilà," she announced, and threw it open.

The room had been stripped of all furniture, and fluorescent lights had been placed overhead. Against one wall, a row of stand-up mirrors had been placed and there was a barre. "My dad installed it as an early Christmas present. Do you like it?" She looked at me anxiously.

I looked around the room enviously. "This is wonderful."

Relieved, Leah whirled across the floor. "We can use it any time we need to."

Thomas went over to the cassette player and turned it on. "Well," he said, warming up to the music.

"Well what?" I asked, shrugging out of my jacket.

Leah started her own warm-up. "Are you coming back to school with us?"

I limbered up as well. "I'm still working on it."

I think Thomas was more worried than even I was When he was anxious, he looked like the scarecrow from the *Wizard of Oz* trying to hatch a thought. "But what will you do if you can't?"

"You just have to." Amy stiffened up, trying to capture Madame's imperial dignity. " 'What the violin is to the musician, a dancer's body is to a dancer.' "

If I hadn't been so nervous myself, I would have laughed. "I won't flab out," I said. "I'll practice on my own."

Thomas assumed the first position with his heels together, feet turned out in a straight line, and Leah did the same. "It's one thing to do it during the holidays . . . "

Amy joined them in raising her arms. "Because you know what I will say if you come back to class sloppy," she said in imitation of Madame. And she prodded him in back.

Thomas started to bend his knees in a demi-plié with Amy and Leah. "But trying to do it on your own. I mean repeating everything over and over. It's boring."

"And no one to correct you." Amy straightened gracefully, performing the relevé best of the three.

"It's only temporary, you guys. So just chill out," I snapped. I banged the buttons on the player so that the old tape stopped and popped out.

Thomas exchanged glances with Leah and Amy. "She's got the temperament to go with the talent of a soloist," Thomas teased.

Squatting, I sorted through the tapes of music and slipped a new one in. There was enough of a lead on the tape so that I could assume my place at the barre before the first notes began. And I let the golden sounds from the piano wash all of my troubles from my mind. All there was to think about was the music and slowly, patiently teaching my body to assume the positions and poses that I wanted.

Madame had explained that ballet was like a language that our bodies and not our tongues spoke. And each position was a word in that language. "And so," she had said, "you must learn to speak clearly and precisely and gracefully. And that only comes through much, much practice."

And so I began yet another practice session, moving through a series of knee bends, or demi-pliés to the deeper bends of the grand-pliés. The exercises gradually worked up our legs from the ankles to the knees to the hips. And finally we began sweeping our legs in the battements to the grand battements. On all of the exercises, I was tough on myself, trying to concentrate deeper than the others in all my moves.

I was feeling energetic and sharp when we began the floor exercises. My leaps, I was pleased to note, were still the best; and no one could perform the "step of the cat" like me. If ballet was a language, I would try to turn it into poetry—once I could begin lessons with Madame again.

Christmas came and went. We didn't even have a tree this year. Every penny went to bringing my grandmother from Hong Kong.

For months, Ian had been dropping hints about a set of soldiers he wanted at Toys Я Us. Instead, he got cheap imitations made in China. They were like blobs of plastic with hardly any recognizable details. He had knelt there with the shreds of paper all around him, staring through the clear plastic bag.

Though it bothered both my parents, my dad was the most distressed by Ian's reaction. He seemed as unhappy as Ian, and it took a couple of nudges from Mom before he turned to me. "Here you go, hon." He held out a card to me.

I had asked for season tickets to the San Francisco Ballet—cheap ones high up in the second balcony. However, after seeing what Ian had gotten, I had my own doubts as I took it. Slipping an index finger beneath the sealed flap, I tore the envelope open and took out the card. "To our sweet daughter." Well, at least Mom and Dad had sprung for a Hallmark. Opening it, I saw there was just one ticket.

"They tell me it's one of the best seats in the house," Mom said. "Third row center, in the orchestra."

To *The Nutcracker.* The words blazed at me from the stiff cardboard. It was the last thing I wanted.

Mom had written something on the card, and I read it:

"To Robin, who is so thoughtful and sweet and sacrificing."

As if I had a choice.

Mom prompted us: "Merry Christmas, Ian and Robin."

Remembering my manners, I closed the card. "Thank you," I said. I couldn't help contrasting my present with the practice room Leah had received.

"Thank you," Ian mumbled.

Mom sprang to her feet as if she were eager to escape. "Now who's for some pancakes?"

"What about *your* presents?" I asked.

Dad clapped his hands together nervously. "We decided not to give each other presents this year."

And I had been feeling bad for getting just one ticket. "Well, there's still mine," I said. To Mom I gave a pot holder. And to Dad I gave a crocheted diamond-shaped coaster. "You slip it under your cup," I explained to him.

He squinted at it. "But what colors are they?"

"Orange and blue, the colors of your old school." Mom laughed. "It's a good thing you let me put your clothes out to dress, or who knows what you'd wear?"

"Now mine," Ian insisted.

After we all admired his handmade cards, we had a breakfast of pancakes and syrup, and I salved the hurt with the money I had received from Nana. She had sent a check for twenty dollars each to Ian and me.

We called her right away. She had a voice warm as butter melting on a hot muffin. "I just didn't know what to buy you, honey," she said. "Your father sent me a copy of the videotape. You're growing up so fast."

I laughed. "I hope not too much. There's not much call for tall dancers."

"You dance so lovely." Nana became apologetic. "I know this will sound funny, but it made me just ache inside when I saw your solo."

I tried to be modest. "You're just prejudiced, Nana."

"Well that's a grandmother's privilege," Nana insisted. "I'm going to show the tape at my next bridge night."

I took a secret pleasure in Nana's pride as I turned her over to Ian. When he was done, it was Dad and Mom's turn.

After that, I tried to dial up Amy and Leah but only got their answering machines. I'd forgotten that Amy was at her aunt's and Leah was with her father for Christmas.

Thomas, though, was home, as I knew he would be. He and his mother never seemed to go anywhere or do anything. "Merry Christmas, Thomas," I said, trying to sound cheerful.

After years of regular and ballet school, though, he knew me too well. "What's wrong, Robin?"

Compared to his home life, mine was a piece of cake. "I guess Christmas wasn't quite what I expected."

"Is it ever? Did you know that the number of

suicides jumps at this time of year?" He was a fount of morbid statistics.

I played with the telephone cord. "Gee, you always know how to cheer me up."

"It's a talent," he chuckled. "You're either born with it or you never get it. So as the official dispenser of holiday cheer, would you like your present now?"

I hesitated. "It . . . it isn't anything dead, is it?" With Thomas, you never knew. His mother eked out a living drawing pictures for biology textbooks, so their apartment was filled with animal skulls and stuffed animals.

"No," he tried to assure me. "It's strictly magnetized iron dust."

"What?" I asked.

"A cassette," Thomas explained. "I bought the blank tape and Amy and I made it on Leah's stereo."

If Amy and Leah were involved, I guessed I was safe from one of his macabre pranks. "Sure, bring it over."

I got an envelope and slipped the *Nutcracker* ticket into it. With no definite date for ballet school, it would be too painful to see it now. I was going to wait in the living room, but Dad was there with the football game blaring. The kitchen was no haven because Mom was in there, working at her calculator and studying the figures on the tape. So I wound up waiting in my bedroom.

Since Thomas lived nearby, it didn't take long for

him to reach us. When I heard the doorbell ring, I shouted, "I'll get it!"

Ian was off in his room, playing with his new soldiers. As I passed, I could hear him make shooting noises and explosions.

When I opened the door, Thomas held out a brightly wrapped box. *"Joyeux Noel."*

"Merry Christmas," I wished him, and stepped back. "Come on in."

He shook his head. "Christmas is a family time."

I was eager for friendly company. "Visit for a little while."

Thomas had a funny little smile. It was more like a quick twitch of his lips. If you blinked your eyes, you could miss it. It was almost as if he were afraid that anyone would discover he was happy. "No, I got family stuff myself, you know."

So much family stuff that he could leave it and come right over. But, I knew how proud he could be, so I didn't call his bluff. "Sure, I know how it is. Here then." I thrust the envelope at him. "This is for you or Leah or Amy. You'll have to toss a coin to see who gets it."

He took the envelope and held it to his head. "And the answer is: camel sweat."

I grinned at the feeble joke. "Give me a call tomorrow."

"Yeah, tomorrow." He raised his hand in farewell

and was already taking the steps two at a time down toward the street.

I stood in the doorway and watched the forlorn figure lope away before I shut the door. Then I took my present to my room.

The box was wrapped in shiny red foil with a bow of iridescent ribbon. The little card attached said: "So you won't get sloppy." It was signed by Thomas, Leah, and Amy, and Thomas had drawn cartoons of the trio as bloated blimps.

Normally I'm very careful unwrapping presents. I think the anticipation is half the pleasure of a gift, but I felt so frustrated with the day that I tore off the paper. It was a tape cassette, just as Thomas had said. On the card that went with the case, I saw that Amy had written out the songs in her neat hand. It was all my favorite tunes, and it finished with the Sugar Plum Fairy solo.

Taping their card to my wall, I popped their gift into my old cassette player. The speakers were really too small, so the music sounded a little tinny, but I shut my eyes, remembering what it was like to step into the light. To be something beautiful.

All too soon, Dad was knocking at my door to tell me we had to go to the family party. We were meeting that afternoon at a restaurant with the rest of Mom's family.

As soon as we came through the restaurant door,

our cousin Harold came running up the aisle in a new red sports coat and blue shorts. He was about Ian's age and height. "Look what I got," he said, holding up a huge toy.

"Lucky," Ian said. From his envious expression, I knew it must be the latest fad among boys his age— and probably very expensive.

Harold hefted the toy. "My dad had to go to a dozen toy stores to find it. He drove all over the Bay Area." Knowing his father, Uncle Georgie, he'd probably had some flunky find it for him, but I held my tongue. "What'd you get?" he asked Ian.

Ian jammed his hands into his jeans pockets. "Some stuff."

Our other cousins weren't any better. There were either new clothes or new toys or new watches. Though I felt like wincing sometimes, I managed to make it through the whole luncheon.

When we got home, I cornered Mom in the kitchen. "Mom, when can I go back to ballet classes?"

Mom carried the tea kettle to the sink. "We'll talk about it when your grandmother comes."

I wasn't going to let her put me off. "And when is that?"

"I told you there's red tape and all sorts of bureaucratic nonsense." Twisting the faucet knob, she began to fill the kettle.

I leaned over so she had to look at me. "It seems like we're making more sacrifices than our cousins."

She pressed her lips together thinly. "I've had more advantages than my brothers. It's only fair. I got to come over, while they stayed in Hong Kong. Georgie got sick from rickets, and Eddy got polio."

"When are you going to stop feeling guilty?" Dad asked. "You've paid them back." Neither of us had heard him come in. "You've brought them over and paid for their college educations."

"They're my little brothers," Mom insisted, "so the subject is closed."

"But—" Dad began.

"It's closed," Mom said through her teeth. "You knew how important my family was to me when we got married."

"What about Robin and Ian?" Dad demanded. "Aren't they family too? I don't like being the cheapskate at Christmas while your brothers play Santa Claus."

Mom stood as if posing with the kettle. "Ian understands. He even gave me his check from Nana to help bring over his other grandmother."

"Was it his idea or yours?" Dad asked quietly.

Mom ignored him and looked at me. "What about you, Robin?"

"Elaine, you're going too far," Dad objected.

"Don't aggravate me, Gilbert." Mom banged the kettle onto the stove burner.

Dad and I both knew it was serious when she used his formal name. I looked at Dad, silently pleading with him for help, but he just raised his handmade coaster sadly. "Well, I guess it's time to try out my gift with a cup of tea."

Mom went to the cupboard. "Do you want a cup, Robin?"

"No, thanks," I barely choked out as I held out Nana's check and left.

I sat on my bed, listening to our flat. In his room, Ian was still making war noises. In the living room, Dad was watching a football game. Faintly I could hear the click and whirl of the tape on Mom's calculator as she went over figures yet again.

A room should look different on Christmas, with boxes and torn paper and strips of curling ribbon. Instead, my room looked depressingly the same. As I looked around gloomily, I saw the card from my friends.

"So you won't get sloppy."

The caricatures had made me smile at first, but now they almost made me cry. With no definite time for ballet lessons to begin, I suddenly felt so empty inside and out. I had been to a fun house once. In it, there had been a ride that was a big circular platform. At Dad's urging, we all had lain down with the others. When the platform had begun spinning, we all went flying off and landed on the padded floor.

I had this awful feeling that I was on that ride now,

but there was no floor to catch me and I would just go on falling through space, farther and farther.

As I stared at the three little blimps, the sorrow felt as sharp as a knife. And suddenly I knew what I had to do.

I'd keep my word to Amy, Leah, and Thomas. If I couldn't have classes, I would practice on my own. I would keep my body ready for Madame's lessons.

Finally I couldn't take it anymore. If I didn't get to dance, I would burst. So I got my old cassette player and went down the back stairs to the ground-floor garage. Our neighbors in the other flat, the Aguilars, had parked their Lincoln inside, but Dad had left our old Honda outside on the driveway after we came back from the restaurant. I supposed he would put it inside later.

Running parallel to the floor for the length of the wall was a pipe. I supposed it was for water. I judged it critically for the distance. It would make a good makeshift barre.

Slipping the cassette into the player, I turned it on. As I began to warm up to the songs, I felt calmer. In the back of my mind, I could hear Madame talking to us as we limbered up.

"It is natural to dance," she had often told us. "Before a baby can hold a brush, a baby can move to music. So it is natural to dance, but the steps to classical ballet are not natural. A dancer must repeat the steps over and over until position and movement are instinctive. And what is unnatural becomes natural. For classical ballet is the highest expression of dance."

Sometimes Thomas and Amy said Madame was too pompous, but now I held on to her sayings like a drowning girl to a rope.

I repeated them over and over to myself as I did the barre work. And I was still thinking of Madame when I set my feet in the third position, heels of each foot touching the middle of the other. As "Clair de Lune" started, I began a demi-plié—and felt myself overbalance, with my knees out of line with my ankles. It was one of the simplest things that beginners mastered, and yet I was blowing even that. It seemed hopeless without Madame. But yet I forced myself to go on.

I raised my leg until the ankle touched the side of my supporting knee. It was hard to do without the support of the barre. However, I told myself to try to be graceful as I completed the move. That was better. I was sure even Madame would have approved.

And as I swung my body into an arabesque, I felt my muscles stretch in a familiar pattern that felt good. The first time I did my exercises, I always felt a kind of pleasure whenever I did something right. It was with repetition that the exercises would grow boring.

As I began to slide across the floor of the garage in a glissade, I knew I was getting sloppy. A glance at my watch told me that it was too early to stop yet, so I pictured Madame in front of me again. "Faster, Robin. Faster," I imagined her saying with a frown. And I forced my worn-out legs to be quicker.

As I sprang into the "step of the cat," the *pas de chat*, I could hear her telling me, "Higher, Robin. Higher."

And because I had been sloppy, I made myself repeat the exercise. By the time I was finished, I knew it had not been my best practice, but it hadn't been my worst either. And it had certainly been my most thorough. So, even if Madame would not have praised me for what I had just done, she would not have scolded me. If I could keep practicing with the same effort, I would not disgrace myself when I began lessons again.

As long as I could dance, I would be all right.

· FOUR ·

The Arrival

So my ballet lessons and my life in general got put on hold for a while.

I had tried to put *The Nutcracker* out of my mind until a couple of days after Christmas. Mom poked her head into my room and stared at me as I lay on the bed. "Shouldn't you be getting ready for *The Nutcracker?*"

Thomas had won the toss for the ticket, but I wasn't about to tell Mom. "I almost forgot."

Mom gave an affectionate shake of her head. "How could you forget something like that?"

So I wound up getting dressed and wandering around the neighborhood until the performance ended.

The next day Thomas himself came by to present me with the program. "You were a much better Morning Butterfly," he insisted loyally.

"Liar, but thanks for saying that," I said, and moved to kiss him.

Embarrassed, he clapped a hand to his cheek. And then, as he usually did when he felt uncomfortable, he turned it all into a joke. Looking down, he examined himself. "Nope, still a frog."

Ballet classes began a week after Christmas, and it hurt not to be going with Amy and Leah and Thomas to Madame's. Amy was almost as impatient as I was. As the oldest in her family, she was used to organizing people's lives.

"When are you coming back?" she demanded. "We have a special treat planned for Madame." Madame, like a lot of Russians, celebrated January 6, the Feast of the Epiphany, as her Christmas. It was the day when the Magi were supposed to have visited the Christ child.

I thought of my promise to Mom about not telling. "Soon, I hope."

"Madame is always saying how much she misses you," Thomas said. Thomas always preferred to talk about his own feelings by reporting what other people felt.

It wasn't like him to be sentimental, so I expected him to turn it into some sort of joke; but for once he was perfectly sincere.

"Tell her I miss her, too," I mumbled.

"I just don't understand why you can't come back," Leah said worriedly.

I hadn't counted on my friends' curiosity when I made the promise to Mom. "I just can't go into it, okay?"

Thomas, bless his soul, saw the exasperated expression on my face. "Just come back soon," he whispered to me. "Class isn't the same without you."

Of course, I did my exercises faithfully every day—though I hated them. Moving my legs through the different positions over and over was boring.

I thought I might be able to make up in quantity what I lost in quality. So I did ballet until my legs ached. That was when I was most likely to lose my concentration and do something sloppy. And when I made a mistake, I made myself repeat a whole practice routine. When my toes hurt, I ignored the pain. It was probably a result of my practicing on concrete.

And if I felt myself begin to feel tired or bored, I reminded myself of that last dance recital when I had made the audience mine. One day soon, I'd have another chance, and I wanted to be ready when that evening came.

It was just that I still had all this energy inside that I used to work off in Madame's classes. It got so that I did little dance steps the way others scribbled. Once when I was shopping in the supermarket with Mom and Ian, I began going on pointe as I held on to the cart.

Mom did her best to ignore what I was doing.

"Robin, did you investigate the math club like I suggested?"

"I'm not going to be an accountant, Mom," I said vehemently as I danced.

Mom picked a box of cereal from a shelf. "What about sports, then? You can work off some of that excess energy." She went on to suggest a dozen after-school activities.

"They're distractions to a dancer," I said, spinning.

Mom dumped the box into the cart, closing her eyes in embarrassment. "Please, Robin, darling. For once act normal."

"Can't you stop?" Ian complained. "You're giving me a headache."

I was not about to let them forget. "Dance is my life," I said, and to demonstrate I pirouetted down an aisle.

The months piled on one after another. Sometimes there was something wrong with the paperwork in Hong Kong, sometimes in America. And it always seemed to cost more money because that was the grease that kept the bureaucratic machine running.

I pestered my parents about the lessons just as hard as my friends pestered me. Worst of all, I continued to grow taller. I tried to tell my body to stop, but it wouldn't. It just kept stretching. And Mom grumbled so much about buying new clothes and shoes that I was afraid to ask her for new toe shoes. I was afraid that if I said anything, Mom would tell me to stop practicing rather than buy me new shoes. Instead, I made do with my old ones even though they were now so cramped that I thought I was going to split them.

When my toes started to curl downward in a funny way, I assumed it came from dancing in tight shoes and on a concrete floor. When I strapped them down with adhesive tape, it helped some, though they still hurt a little.

But now when I tried to leap into the air, there was always a little pain when I landed. And the higher I leapt, the more I paid for it. It made me feel even more earthbound.

I couldn't wait for that Friday in October when Grandmother would arrive. It was unusually sunny that day. The light swept over the park grass, across the busy street, and onto our living room rug. In that bright, warm rectangle of light, I did my ballet exercises, using the top of a table as makeshift barre. It was such a pretty day that it was easy for me to forget the little aches and pains in my feet.

Then, with a giggle, Ian started to dodge in and out between my legs. I had long ago given up telling him to stop. I simply ignored him now.

When we heard a car stop outside, Ian rushed to the window. "She's here! She's here!" he shouted excitedly. "*Paw-paw's* here!" *Paw-paw* is Chinese for maternal grandmother. He started to race toward the stairs, but I caught him.

"Slow down, or you'll break your neck," I said, and took his hand.

His little legs were still so short that he had to take the steps one at a time. Since we lived in a third-floor flat, there was a flight of stairs to the entranceway and another flight to the street itself.

Behind me, I could hear Mom murmuring to herself as she went over everything. She wanted to make sure we hadn't forgotten anything.

As we moved down the last steps to the street, I saw a pile of luggage and cardboard boxes wrapped in rope. "Is that all Grandmother's?" I whispered to my mother. I didn't see how it would all fit into my bedroom.

Mom laughed. "We're lucky she had to leave her furniture behind in Hong Kong."

Ian let go of my hand. "Do you need any help, Daddy?" he asked.

"This is the last." Dad's brown head rose out of our car trunk. In his arms, he had another box wrapped in rope, which he added to the stack on the sidewalk. "See," he announced to the car, "everything's here."

The car door opened, and Grandmother slid across the backseat. "Are you sure?" Grandmother demanded. She was a small woman in a silk padded jacket and black slacks. On her small feet, she wore a pair of quilted cotton slippers shaped like boots, with furred tops that hid her ankles. Resting across her knees were a pair of carved black canes.

Dad looked both sweaty and harassed. "Wait," he said, and slammed the trunk shut.

But Grandmother was already getting to her feet using her canes. "I'm not helpless," she insisted to Dad.

Ian was relieved. "She speaks English," he whispered to Mother.

"She worked for a British family for years," Mom explained in a low voice.

"What's wrong with her legs?" I asked her.

"They've always been that way. And don't mention it," she said. "She's sensitive about them."

I was instantly curious. "But what happened to them?"

"Wise grandchildren wouldn't ask," Mom warned.

Grandmother had pulled her hair back into a bun behind her head, emphasizing its pear shape. Her thick lips moved as she began to count her belongings. "Are you sure you got everything?"

"Yes, they're all there." Dad closed the rear car door.

Mom stepped around us and walked over to her mother. "I'm so glad you're here, Mother," she said with a formal bow.

Grandmother turned slowly with the help of her

canes, but the smile froze on her face. She gazed past us toward the steps leading to the entranceway. Through our front door, she probably saw the next stairway. "Why do you have to have so many steps?"

Though Mom was in her forties, she sounded as meek as a child. "I'm sorry."

Dad tried to change the subject. "That's Robin, and that little monster is Ian."

"*Joe sun, Paw-Paw,*" I said. "Good morning, Grandmother." It was afternoon, but that was the only Chinese I knew, and I had been practicing it.

Mother had coached us on a proper Chinese greeting for the last two months; but I decided to also give her the same kind of howdy that I gave my other grandmother, Nana.

But when I tried to put my arms around her and kiss her, she stiffened in surprise. "Nice children don't drool on people," she snapped at me.

Ian, though, bowed, just as we had been drilled. "*Joe sun, Paw-Paw.*" And then, because Ian thought anything worth doing was worth repeating, he bowed a second time.

Grandmother brightened in an instant. "He has your eyes," she said to Mom.

"Elaine, why don't you show her room to her," Dad suggested.

Mom bent and hefted Ian into her arms. "It was Robin's room, so I hope you don't mind the furnishings."

Grandmother didn't even thank me as she stumped after Mom. She was too busy trying to coax a smile from Ian, who was staring at her over Mom's shoulder.

I was going to follow them, but Dad stopped me. "Robin, I need you to watch your grandmother's things until I finish bringing them up."

Taking a suitcase in each hand, he caught up with them at the foot of the first staircase.

Grandmother's climb was long, slow, and laborious. *Thump, thump, thump.* Her canes struck the boards as she slowly mounted the steps. It sounded like the steady beat of a mechanical heart. It was hard to see how she had ever made that heroic trek across China on those wobbly legs.

While I waited for Dad, I inspected Grandmother's pile of belongings. In their webbing of tight cords, the boxes had words in Chinese and English. Hong Kong was as exotic to me as America was to Grandmother. Putting a hand on one, I bent slowly in a port de bras forward. As I leaned over next to it, I could smell its exotic scent, and my imagination immediately pictured sunlit waters lapping at picturesque docks.

When Dad returned to the sidewalk, his face was red from the exertion. "Don't you ever get tired of doing your ballet exercises?"

I swept my leg back and forth in a grand battement. When I felt myself make a mistake, I told myself to do two dozen more. "Madame Oblamov would want me to practice every day."

He winced as I crossed and uncrossed my legs rapidly, keeping the feet parallel to one another. "Doesn't that hurt?"

"When I started," I said. I almost smiled when I thought of my first awkward attempts.

"Why do you punish yourself that way?" he asked as he watched.

I tried to think of an answer while I exercised. Why did I? Was it for the applause? Frankly, there were a lot easier ways to gain the approval of other people.

I tried to remember what I had felt during that last performance—it seemed like an age ago. "I like being graceful." If only for a few minutes.

"There are other ways of being graceful," he said. "I'd dislocate both my hip joints if I tried that."

And I realized that I had done a poor job of explaining. "It's not so much about me. It's being part of something." I stopped, frustrated at trying to explain that feeling I'd had onstage.

Crouching, he used the cords to lift a box in each hand. "Well, I guess some of us have it and some of us don't. I just wish I had half your energy."

I had waited for this day, not only for Grandmother's sake, but for my own; and I couldn't control myself any longer. "Now that Grandmother's here, when can I begin my ballet lessons again?"

Dad turned toward the house. "We'll see, hon."

I had been expecting some date, any date. If I was absent much longer, Madame might start me over again with a beginners' class. "But you said I had to give up the lessons so we could bring her from Hong Kong. Well, she's here."

Dad hesitated and then put the boxes down. "Try to understand, hon. We've got to get your grandmother set up here. That's going to take even more money. Don't you want your room back?"

Poor Dad. He looked tired and worried. I should have shut up, but I loved ballet almost as much as I loved him. "But when can I start again? Can't you even guess?"

"Soon. I promise." He looked guilty as he picked up the boxes and struggled toward the stairs.

He managed to avoid me for the rest of the day because we had to get ready for the family get-together that evening. Though Uncle Eddy and Uncle Georgie each had a house, we wound up holding the party in our flat. When the four families squeezed in, I started to know how a sardine felt.

When Dad made the dinner run, I volunteered to help him because I thought it would give me a chance to work on him one-on-one. However, he outsmarted me by corralling Uncle Georgie.

"Georgie, how about giving me a lift?" he asked. "I hate to give up my parking space."

Uncle Georgie loved to show off his black Mercedes. "Sure thing," he said, fishing out his keys.

Uncle Georgie and Uncle Eddy did not have British accents because they had come over at a younger age. Mom had worked hard to be able to sponsor them, and then had supported them for years while they went to school. She'd only gone back to evening school once they'd gotten married and moved out.

Dad had parked down the block to leave the driveway open for somebody, and Uncle Georgie had grabbed the opportunity. It took him about five minutes to turn off all the alarms. While he worked on entering his car, I saw that his license plates had just "888."

As I got in, I could smell the leather upholstery. "Uncle Georgie, if you're going to have specialized plates, why not use the name of your business?"

Uncle Georgie gave me a look as if I were the dumbest child in creation—though his kids were just as Americanized as me. In fact, none of us grandchildren could speak to Grandmother in Chinese.

"Because in Chinese numerology, a triple eight is lots of luck," he explained, and shut the door gently.

Uncle Georgie's car had power everything. When Dad spotted the space in front of the Dragon River, Uncle Georgie pulled in easily, swinging the wheel with just his right hand while he kept his left arm draped over the car door. However, because he didn't have a quarter for the meter, Dad wound up treating to the parking.

When we went in, Uncle Georgie tried to order in Chinese, but the waiter looked puzzled and said something else. They spoke back and forth for a couple of minutes before Uncle Georgie picked up a menu and grumbled, "The idiot speaks the wrong dialect."

He wound up pointing at items just like I have to when I go to a Chinese restaurant. When his finger jabbed at lobster, Dad scratched his head. "Isn't that pretty expensive?"

"How often do you get reunited with your mother?" And he ordered four.

While we waited for the restaurant to cook our order, Dad asked, "So how's your business, Georgie?"

Uncle Georgie selected a toothpick from the dispenser on the counter. "Oh, great. Hired three new people last month."

He set the toothpick in one corner of his mouth, and I watched it flick up and down while he bragged about his business. He was still boasting when the waiter brought out our order. All the little white cartons were arranged inside a cardboard box like blocks.

When the waiter presented the bill, Uncle Georgie reached grandly for it; but then the toothpick dropped from his lips. "I guess I got a little carried away." Glancing up at the waiter, he pulled out his wallet and got out his credit card.

"They only take cash, Georgie," Dad said.

Uncle Georgie checked his wallet. There were only a couple of very tattered singles there. "You should have warned me so we could go to another place."

Dad wearily reached for his wallet. He looked as if he was trying to figure out what this would do to our budget. "Let me get this one. It's not every day you get reunited with your mother-in-law."

Uncle George sheepishly restored his credit card to his wallet. "I'll pay you back."

"Sure you will," Dad said stiffly.

"I will," Uncle Georgie insisted.

As Dad drew some bills from his wallet, he couldn't resist digging it in: "Like you did for the poker party?"

Uncle Georgie sat back. "Oh, yeah. I forgot about that."

"Or the time . . ." Dad named a couple of other lapses of memory as he paid the bill.

Uncle Georgie frowned. "What do you do? Keep an account book? Will you take a check?" He started to reach inside his coat and swore. "My checks are at home. See, I do all my business by plastic."

Dad got back his change and left several dollars as a tip. "It's okay. You can get me next time." From the way he said it, he didn't think Uncle Georgie would ever remember.

Before the waiter could snatch up his tip from the table, Uncle Georgie took a dollar from it and handed it back to Dad. "That's enough. How do you ever expect to get rich?"

"I don't know, Georgie," Dad sighed.

"I'll get the door." Uncle Georgie quickly skipped up from the table. He was against lifting anything heavy, from boxes of food to checks. Poor Dad was left to heave up the box of food.

"Let me help, Daddy," I said, taking two cartons by their handles.

"I don't know what I'd do without you, sweetheart." He puffed as he moved toward the door.

After what Uncle Georgie had done to him, I would have felt like I was picking on Dad to ask about my ballet lessons. As I followed him out of the restaurant, I decided to give him a reprieve. But tomorrow I would have my reckoning yet.

FIVE

The Reckoning

I was ready to go to bed early, but I had to entertain my cousins. I was so groggy when we finally got rid of them that I started to head for my old room.

"Who's there?" Grandmother called from the darkness.

"Sorry, *Paw-Paw*. It's just Robin. I got turned around." I crept into Ian's room, where a mattress had been put on the floor for me. Ian was already snoring softly as I lay down in my clothes.

When I woke up the next morning, Ian was already gone. I glanced at the Batman clock and saw it was nine. Yawning, I staggered out to the hallway. I was surprised to see boxes piled haphazardly.

When I went to ask Dad what was happening, I found him busily lugging Grandmother's old clunky stereo out of a box. "We have a stereo," I said.

"But it won't play Grandmother's records. They were recorded at 78 rpm's," Dad explained, putting it down in the living room.

When he brought out her record collection from another box, I started to go through them, but they were all in Chinese. "Is there anyone I know?"

"I doubt it." Dad laughed. He hooked up the stereo and tried a record as an experiment.

I couldn't believe what I was hearing. "It sounds awful."

Dad laughed because usually he was the one complaining about my music. "Chinese music has thirteen tones—five more than western music. It's just different."

I backed away from the speakers. "I wish she'd left it back in Hong Kong."

Dad straightened. "I know you don't mean that."

"No," I said guiltily.

When we heard the *thump, thump, thump,* Dad put a finger to his lips. It was Grandmother, walking with her canes. I had begun to hate the sound.

"Thank you," she said.

She wore soft slippers shaped like boots so they covered her feet to the ankle. Each step she took, she paused. "Hello," she said to Dad. "Hello," she said to me.

"How did you sleep last night?" Dad asked politely as he took her elbow to support her.

"The bed was too soft," she said. "But that's all right. I can put up with the aches."

"I'll get a sheet of plywood today and put it beneath the mattress," he promised, and helped her sit down. "I got your stereo set up."

"I listen to it all the time. What is on there?" She pointed a cane at the television.

Dad turned off the stereo and then turned on the television. "I don't know what's on," he said as he crouched by the dial.

The shows clicked across the screen steadily as he changed the channels. He would pause at each for a moment and look back questioningly at Grandmother. And every time she would shake her head after a while. "Too hard," she said. I assumed it meant it was too hard to understand.

Dad scratched his head. "Let's see. If I remember right, there's a Chinese channel."

As a Chinese couple appeared on the screen, Grandmother declared happily, "Just like at home."

Satisfied, Dad folded his arms and stepped back in triumph. "I knew I'd find it."

The show was subtitled but in Chinese. I watched the words painted in white flow across the screen. "Why does it have Chinese words too?"

"In China, there are different dialects," Grandmother explained. "People might speak the words in many ways, but the written characters are always the same. Even if a Chinese person doesn't understand the dialect the actors speak in the movie, she can read the Chinese subtitles. Can you?"

I had to shake my head. "No, I'm sorry."

Grandmother shook her head in disgust. "All you grandchildren are the same." She nodded toward my T-shirt. "And look at your clothes."

I fingered the hem. "What's wrong with the way I dress?"

Grandmother gave a shiver. "It's too cold."

Since we were in T-shirts and she was in a sweater, I looked at her in surprise. "Do you want me to get you a coat?"

"My hand." She held up her stiff fingers and said something in Chinese. "I forgot the English word."

Dad made an educated guess. "You've got rheumatism?"

"Yes," Grandmother said. "Can you make it warmer?"

"I'll turn up the heat." As he fiddled with the thermostat, I went over to him.

"Can we afford the heating bill?" I asked anxiously.

"She comes from a tropical climate, Robin. And to top it off she's got rheumatism." With a forced smile, he turned up the temperature. Instantly the furnace kicked in. "We don't have any choice, honey."

Ian came in that moment. "My cartoon's on."

Dad intercepted him as he headed for the television. "Your grandmother's watching her show."

"But I always watch my cartoon now," Ian complained.

Grandmother pointed a cane at the television. "You watch. You learn," she said.

Ian listened uncomprehendingly to the Chinese. "I think I'll go play," he said.

I made my escape a moment later. There were more boxes in the hallway now, and when I inspected one closer, I was shocked to find that it contained the dolls I kept on top of my bureau. When Mom came out of my old room, I asked, "What's going on?"

"Grandmom needs the room for her things," Mom explained, and set the box outside.

Shocked, I followed Mom back inside my old room. "But sleeping with Ian was only supposed to be temporary," I protested.

Mom paused before the bureau. "There have been complications, Robin. Eddy and Georgie think she should stay here for a while. They can't take her yet."

I couldn't believe my ears. "But they both have big houses."

Mom held on to the drawer knobs as if she needed support. "The family thinks it would be too much of a shock if she moved too soon."

Helplessly I watched Mom open the drawer and begin to take out my things. "I already cleared out one drawer for her," I complained.

Mom kept dumping my things into boxes relentlessly. "That seemed like enough when we thought she would be here for a couple of days. Now take that box to Ian's room."

Ian didn't like the idea any better. "Where am I going to play?" he demanded as I began to stack up my boxes.

Between his stuff and mine, there were now only narrow lanes to the beds.

"I don't like it any better than you do," I said and set my box on top of a stack.

The final straw came when Mom began to take down my posters. "I'm already living out of boxes," I argued.

It was safe to talk because Grandmother was still watching Chinese television in the front of the apartment. Because she was hard of hearing, she had the sound turned way up.

"Grandmom wants to put up some special pictures," Mom explained.

It was the first I knew that Grandmother might like rock stars. "Who?" I wondered.

"People who will watch over her and help her get better." Mom began to roll up the posters.

"Like angels?" I asked.

"Chinese angels," Mom corrected, and handed the roll of posters to me.

It was the final straw for Ian when I began to hang up my posters. "I don't want to see their ugly faces."

"I don't want to look at the Wolf Warriors." I went on sticking up the posters with masking tape. "If I have to make sacrifices, so do you."

When Ian tried to take the poster off the wall, I shoved him away. But he was still holding on to a corner, and the poster tore in half. Ian fell and knocked over a stack of boxes, spilling my toys and things all over. "Mom!" we both shouted.

Looking harried, Mom darted into the room. "What's wrong?" She panted.

Since each of us felt put upon, we both complained about the other's crimes at the same time. "Quiet!" Mom yelled. She put her hands to her face and sat down on the nearest box. Her shoulders began to shake, and at first we stared at her. Her sob came muffled through her hands.

"She's crying," Ian said softly.

Mom almost never cried. She was the kind of person who always checked the last pages of a book before she bought it. She never went to a movie unless someone else could tell her if it ended happily.

I put my hand on her shoulder. "Mom?" I asked.

"I'll be okay." She sniffed.

"Elaine." Grandmother's voice came floating down the hallway over the sound of the television.

Hastily Mom wiped her eyes on her sleeves and got up. "Yes, Mama," she called, and hurried down the hallway.

I was so caught up in my own problems that I hadn't thought about Mom. I tried to think how I would feel if I hadn't seen my mother all those years. I'd be worried and impatient too. And I knew now was not the time to talk to her about ballet lessons. I might even have to put it off for yet another day.

Ian got up and handed me his half of the poster. "Maybe we can tape it together."

"It's okay. He was getting kind of boring." I began to pick up the things that had gotten scattered during Ian's fall.

"You can put up your other posters," Ian said.

"Thanks."

I wanted to be good. I really did. But when I went into my room and saw the strange pictures on the wall and the pills and bottles on the bureau top, it didn't seem like my room anymore. It didn't smell like my room either. The odor wasn't unpleasant, but it was strong—like the inside of a cedar chest. Then, when I realized I would have to live out of cardboard boxes for a long time, I felt . . . well . . . homeless. It was about that time that I really began to resent Grandmother.

I was starting to feel guilty for thinking those kinds of thoughts, when Mom returned. "Ian, Robin, sit down."

"I already am sitting," I said.

Mom distractedly ran a hand over her forehead. "I meant Ian."

"Why is it always me?" Ian demanded as he plopped down on his bed.

"You both have to be more quiet," Mom said. "Your grandmother was taking a nap in the living room. You woke her up."

"She listens to the television loud," Ian pointed out.

"But it's unexpected noises that wake her," Mom said. "She's had a long flight, honey. And that's harder on someone that old."

"We didn't mean to argue," I said cautiously.

"I mean noise in general." Mom picked up a cap gun from the floor. "And that means no loud, active games, Ian. She needs her rest."

It was Ian's turn to be shocked as Mom began to gather up all of his guns and Nerf balls. "And no listening to the radio loud." She nodded toward the old reconditioned boom box that Dad had bought from Goodwill for Ian. "And no loud television either."

"What are we supposed to do?" Ian asked indignantly.

"Read," Mom said.

"Well, if I can't run around," Ian sulked "then Robin can't do her ballet exercises."

That was a new, chilling thought that hadn't occurred to me. "Maybe I should begin at Madame Oblamov's, then."

Mom dumped all the forbidden toys together. "Not now, Robin."

"But you promised," I said.

"Robin!" Mom's voice got that odd, quivering edge again. As Ian and I both sat petrified, Mom recovered herself. "You can keep doing your lessons in the garage. You'll just have to make do like the rest of us." Gathering up the armful of toys, she left.

I wanted to like *Paw-paw*. She was my grandmother, after all. But it was getting harder and harder.

Evil Brother: Part Twelve

The next day, Monday, Leah, Amy, and Thomas were already hovering by my locker when I got there. "So?" Amy asked when I walked up.

"So what?" I asked as I began to work my combination lock.

"So how'd it go with your grandmother?" Amy demanded impatiently. She was a born busybody.

I slid the lock out. "She got here."

"So do hurricanes," Leah harumphed. "What does that mean?"

I thought over all the indignities and injustices and felt guilty feeling that way. Perhaps she would grow on me. "She's . . . a little different."

Thomas nodded his head sagely. "Ah, I understand."

Annoyed, Leah nudged him with an elbow. "Is there something I missed?"

It was never Thomas's way to use four words when he could use forty, so he got frustrated with me. "Pink tuxedos are different too, but you'll never get me to like them."

"I'll keep that in mind," I said as I jerked the locker door open.

Leah swung the door out wider. "What's wrong with her?" Leah would make a good investigative reporter because she was born to snoop. She might even win a Pulitzer one day—if someone didn't strangle her first.

"She's not quite what I expected," I admitted as I put my book bag inside.

Leah seemed all sad eyes, and with her hollow cheeks, she could have been a poster for some starving children's charity. "My grandmother keeps trying to stuff all these fatty, unhealthy foods down my throat."

Thomas's expressive face grimaced as if he had a terrible pain. "You wouldn't want to meet either of mine unless you like visiting maximum security prisons."

I had already said too much. There were three ways of spreading information instantly: telegraph, telephone, and tell-a-Thomas. "You win the awful-grandmother contest," I said carefully.

"At least you have grandmothers," Amy said wistfully. "Both of mine are dead."

After Amy put things into perspective, the three of us were silent.

Almost guiltily, Amy steered the topic of conversation back to the main track. We all shared a common love that kept us going on when others had dropped out. When one of us got discouraged, the others would encourage her or him so that she or he stayed with ballet. "Did your parents say when you could begin lessons again?"

I had been dreading this moment. "No."

"Why not? Ask them," Leah nudged me. Once she'd sunk her teeth into a topic, she wouldn't let go until I agreed with her. No one ever won an argument with Leah, especially when it was about something as important to her as ballet.

I thought of telling them about the Debt, but I knew that Mom wouldn't want me broadcasting it across the city. Sometimes it wasn't good to have inquisitive friends.

"I tried." I shrugged. "It isn't the right time."

"Make it the right time." Leah folded her arms as if that were exactly what she would do.

So earnest, so worried, Amy was a regular little mother. "You can't let your ballet go."

I got out my books for the next couple of classes. "I'm still practicing at home."

Leah grimly leaned an elbow against another locker. "That's not the same, and you know it."

I had been trying to ignore it up until now. I felt like Leah and Amy were taking turns punching me in the stomach.

I remembered my promise to Mom again, but I just couldn't take it any longer. I needed to complain to someone else. "You can't tell anyone else. Swear?" When my three friends nodded solemnly, I told them, "There just isn't the money." I felt so ashamed that I wished I could huddle up in a ball.

"Why not?" Leah demanded.

"Bringing my grandmother over was expensive, and now there are other expenses." I added, "So you mustn't tell anyone. Especially that part."

Leah, though, was more mystified than ever. "Don't you have uncles? Surely they can help."

"Mom says they have their own expenses right now," I said, but that argument sounded feeble even to me.

"Why do you have to be the only one to sacrifice?" Thomas demanded indignantly.

Why indeed? I wasn't so sure I really understood either. I mean, my family was still renting a flat while my uncles had houses and businesses. Amy, though, was Chinese enough to understand. "Chill," she said to Leah and Thomas. "It's family stuff."

"But—" Leah began to protest.

I shrugged noncommittally and saw that Leah and Thomas still didn't understand.

"Things will work out," said Amy, but she gazed at me with pity. It was the look we gave our other friends who had already quit ballet.

"Sure, you'll be back," Thomas said.

"I will," I insisted, slamming my locker door shut.

"Of course," Amy said, patting me on the shoulder, but Leah and Thomas, I think, had already written me off. Now that I was a casualty, they would close ranks with Amy and march on like soldiers.

I shook off her hand. "I will."

When I got home, I expected Ian to go critical mass and explode in one of his earthshaking tantrums. When he wanted his cartoons, he wanted them now. I could remember one day when he even bit Dad because Dad had wanted to watch a 49ers exhibition game. However, the blowup never came.

Instead, I found Ian and Grandmother watching some Chinese show. Grandmother was sitting in the recliner, watching the actors. Ian sat at the foot of her chair, letting her stroke his hair.

I pivoted to check the screen. From the way the actors were going into hysterics, I assumed the show was some kind of Chinese soap opera.

"Do you understand it, Ian?" I asked.

I realized that his mouth was full only because it took him so long to answer me. He had to free his tongue and then shift to his cheek whatever he was eating. "No."

Ian was like a puppy. He would keep eating if there was something in front of him. And then he would be so surprised and indignant when he got a stomachache. "What're you eating?" I demanded.

"Candy." Tilting back his head and opening his mouth, he stuck out his tongue. The candy looked like a huge shapeless white mass dumped on a pink carpet.

Mom had reduced his candy because the sugar kept him too active. In fact, I didn't know of a stash anywhere in the house. "Where did you get it?" I asked.

The lump disappeared in his mouth. *"Paw-Paw."*

So she had bribed him to watch her shows. I noticed then all the little colored squares of paper on the floor. I supposed they were the wrappers. "You'd better hope Mom doesn't catch you."

"He's too thin," Grandmother said, and stroked his hair affectionately. I saw an open plastic bag filled with little candies.

"Are they good?" I asked.

"Hmmm." Ian nodded his head for emphasis.

I waited for Grandmother to offer me one, but she ignored me for her television show. So I thought I'd drop another hint.

"Are they very sweet?" I asked.

"Hm-mm," Ian hummed.

I felt hurt when Grandmother still didn't take the hint. By now it was a point of honor to get to sample them. "Can I have some?"

Ian leaned his head back to stare up at Grandmother. Reluctantly she dug one square out and handed it to Ian. "These are my favorites. I don't have many. Only these ones I carried with me. I don't know if I can get any more here." She said "here" as if San Francisco were a pigsty at the end of the earth

"Here." Ian pitched the square to me. It slid across the floor and stopped when it hit my shoe.

After the dozen she had stuffed into Ian, it seemed almost insulting to offer me just one piece. I was so irritated that I forgot my curiosity. "No, I think it's too close to dinner. I wouldn't want to spoil my appetite."

Still keeping her eyes on the screen, Grandmother extended her palm. "Don't waste it then."

I felt like pitching it back to her, but my manners got the best of me. Stooping, I swept it into my hand and returned it to Grandmother.

To add insult to injury, Ian put up his hand immediately and she gave him the candy. Feeling angry and humiliated now, I indicated all the discarded wrappers. "Don't forget to pick up your mess," I told Ian, and left. I knew when I wasn't wanted.

At dinner, the conspiracy between them only deepened. On her way home from work, Mom had bought another Chinese meal, so all the dishes were served in wide, shallow Chinese serving bowls. Mom knew all the restaurants that served such huge portions, that it was cheaper than cooking it ourselves.

All through the meal, Grandmother kept picking out tidbits with her chopsticks and putting them on Ian's plate. And Ian kept munching and nibbling away happily.

Over the next few days, she shared other treats with him—preserved plums and apricot wafers and so on. It was as if I didn't exist.

Even when I tried to be nice, I did it wrong. One afternoon I asked her if she'd like some tea.

She sat in the easy chair with her fingers laced over her stomach, while Ian sat by her feet. "Yes, bring me a beaker," she said.

That sounded like an awful lot even if you were very thirsty, but I went into the kitchen anyway and filled the kettle. Once I had put that on the stove, I got out a jug and dumped in several jasmine tea bags. When I finally brought it out to her, she just stared. "What's that?"

I held up the jug. "You said you wanted a beaker."

Ian got up from the floor. "A beaker is a mug," he said, and went in to fetch her one.

"I was wondering what took you so long," she said.

I told myself that it was only a miscommunication and set the jug down on a TV tray near her chair. "Sorry," I mumbled, and left.

I didn't let it get to me because I always had my ballet. When I did the exercises, I could forget my problems and concentrate on something that was in my power to correct. And the more unjust Grandmother was, the harder I did the exercises.

The topper came when I found a doll on the floor of Ian's and my bedroom. When I picked it up, I saw it had a red stripe on one cheek. I wet my fingertip and tried to rub it off, but the ink was indelible.

Holding it by the legs, I stormed out of the room. "What's the meaning of this?" I shouted down the hallway and stumbled over another doll. This one's gown was ruined by a huge splotch of red ink.

Waving them over my head like hatchets, I stormed into the living room, where Grandmother and Ian were watching television while they ate the sweet of the day. "Ian, did you do this?"

With his back against Grandmother's knees, Ian wasn't the least bit afraid of me. "I needed patients for my hospital."

I waved the dolls at him. "But the ink won't come off."

He shrugged. "You never play with them anymore anyway."

I pressed the dolls against my stomach. "But they were mine, Ian. How would you like it if I ruined all of your toys?"

Ian began to unwrap another of his and Grandmother's favorite candies. "Grandmother said I could."

Grandmother did not even bother to look at me. "You're too old to play with dollies."

I was so furious by then that I was beyond speech. I whirled around and left the room before I said some things that I might regret.

When Mom got home, though, I practically ambushed her by the door. "Mom, you have to speak to Uncle Eddy or Uncle Georgie." I held the dolls before her as incriminating evidence. "I have no privacy. Look at what Ian did to my favorite dolls."

Mom closed the door behind her with her heel because in one hand she held a briefcase and in the other she carried a bag of restaurant cartons. "Please, Robin. I've had a very hard day."

I began to back up the steps so I could stay in front of her. "It's not fair, Mom. Ian went through my stuff."

"Tell him not to," Mom said wearily.

"But Grandmother gave him permission," I said in frustration.

"She doesn't mean anything by it," Mom said, slipping around me. "She'll adjust. Just wait and see."

"But," I protested, "in Grandmother's eyes, he can't do anything wrong. She's spoiling him."

"Just give things time," Mom pleaded, and almost ran up the steps to escape me.

Dad wasn't much help either when he got back. "Don't be jealous, honey."

Me, jealous? Well, a little. "If I behaved like that, you'd have dumped me into the bay."

Dad tried to put an arm around my shoulders. "Don't think we didn't want to when you were small. But you turned out pretty okay."

I pulled away. "Well, don't blame me when he turns into an ax murderer."

After that, Ian became a real monster. It was as if my evil little brother had been biding his time all those years. Under Grandmother's protection, he struck and struck again during the next few days. I might just as well have thrown all my stuff out onto the sidewalk. And he did what he liked and ate when he wanted and went to bed whenever he chose.

If it had not been for ballet, I would have gone crazy during those months. Dad was an angel, backing the car out so I could practice in the space next to the neighbor's car.

Ignoring the smell of oil and mildew and the harsh, glaring lightbulb overhead and even the growing pain in my own feet, I threw myself into the exercises. Ballet was my only refuge now. When I danced, I could shrug off the anger like an old, confining costume, and I could escape into a world where I was strong and safe.

SEVEN

The Last Straw

I managed to avoid Madame Oblamov's for almost a year, but then I got a call from Amy, who said she had big news.

I tried to sound cheerful for her sake. "What is it?" I asked over the telephone.

"I don't want to jinx it until I'm sure." On the other end of the line, I could imagine her crossing all of her fingers. "Can you meet me at the ballet school tomorrow?"

I hesitated because I knew it would hurt not to be able to go inside.

Amy, though, guessed the reason behind my silence. "Please. It's really important."

Amy was too serious to lie, so it must be vital. "Sure," I said reluctantly. "I'll meet you outside after class is over."

So that was how I wound up standing outside the

school late one afternoon. Through a window, I heard the piano tinkle inside the studio. As I recognized my routine from the recital, I realized it had been a big mistake to meet Amy here. I should have insisted on going over to her house.

"No, no, no." I heard Madame's voice over the piano. When the music stopped, she announced, "Like so, Thomas." I heard her beat out the steps with her staff. "I know you are tired, but you must prepare for the performance." While I wouldn't have liked her lecture, I felt helpless and flabby standing outside.

The exasperation built inside me until I thought I would explode. If I was a singer, I would have begun singing. Or if I were a poet, I would have put my feelings into a poem. But I was a dancer. So I began to move across the sidewalk, using my arms and legs and body to express my anger—though I was just wearing cheap cloth kung-fu shoes. When I felt a twinge of pain from my toes, I ignored it.

Only this time there was no Ian and no audience to applaud. There was only a man who stared at me as if I were crazy. So I ignored him, but I felt stiff and awkward—like a bug trapped in glue. And the harder I tried to dance, the heavier and uglier I felt.

When the music stopped, I wanted to cry with frustration. As I fought back the tears, I heard Madame Oblamov announce, "So the class is over. Remember what I showed you."

As the rest of the class did its révérence to Madame, I did the same on the sidewalk. Standing there listening to the chatter that marked the end of class, I fought an urge to rush inside and pour out my troubles to Madame. She of all people would understand—but then she might feel obligated to give me lessons for free. And that wasn't right. So I stayed where I was.

If it had been hard for me to hear the class from outside, it was even worse when the students poured out of the school. I had to answer the inevitable questions of how I was and when I was coming back. All right and soon, I mumbled over and over. I hated seeing the pity in their eyes.

In fact, on the way to Leah's with Amy, I felt so exasperated I did a jeté. "Should you be doing that on the sidewalk?" Leah asked me as we walked. "I don't think concrete is good for your feet."

"I don't have that choice," I said. It felt strange not to be loaded down with a heavy bag like theirs.

Leah seemed surprised that I was still doing my exercises. "Oh, you're keeping them up?"

Amy adjusted the sling of her big bag. "Just where have you been doing them?"

I shrugged and executed some jumps. "Wherever I can."

"Well, I hope you do them in your living room on a wooden floor," Amy said.

It all came flowing out of me then, all the petty

slights and insults. "I've been doing it in the garage," I confessed. "I can't make any noise to upset my grandmother." Poor Leah and Amy. They looked as if they'd been caught at the bottom of a waterfall. My tirade continued all the way into Leah's house and all the way into Leah's bedroom.

"I didn't realize it was so bad," Amy said when I was finished.

Leah dumped her bag in a corner. "It makes me glad I'm an only child."

Amy, though, had my mother's perspective. "But she is your grandmother," she said firmly.

I felt bad about forgetting the real purpose of the evening. "Come on. So what's the big news?" I thought Amy was going to tell me that she had been promoted to dance the Arabian Coffee in the Christmas recital. It was about that time when Madame began making the choices for *The Nutcracker*.

"You don't want to hear about me," she said, hesitating.

"Oh, go on," Leah urged as she plopped down on her bed. "Robin will find out anyway."

Amy was a good friend. "I've ranted long enough. What's the good news? I could use some," I encouraged her as I sat beside Leah.

"It's this." She sat down on Leah's bed and opened her bag. From it, she brought a parcel wrapped in tissue paper. Unwrapping the tissue paper, she revealed a new pair of pointe shoes.

She couldn't conceal her excitement and pleasure any longer. "Madame says that I'm ready to go up on pointe."

I was the one who had always been one step ahead of Amy, moving from our intermediate class to the lower advanced class, which danced on pointe. For a moment, I felt a bit of resentment because it wasn't fair, but I stamped it down. She was my friend, and friends wished only the best for one another. "That's wonderful news," I forced myself to say.

"I could even show you what Madame does with me," Amy said enthusiastically, "until you can take lessons again."

And that would make Amy my teacher. It would be like making a photocopy of a photocopy. The more times you do it, the more blurred the picture becomes until you can't recognize it anymore.

"Thank you, but I don't think so," I said, trying to keep my voice level and polite.

Disappointed, Amy put her hands in her lap. "I was looking forward to it."

I knew I had to find some friendlier excuse. "Madame makes her living through the school. If you give me her lessons for free, it would be like stealing from her."

"Oh," Amy said, picking up her shoes, "I never thought about it that way." She cradled them between her hands for a moment.

"Well, at least practice here," Leah urged.

That was too much like charity, and my pride had taken one too many dents that day. I'd been the first one to go up on pointe, and now, while I remained frozen in time, they were catching up. "It's okay during the holidays, when we have no school, but it'd be too awkward now."

"I'm so sorry." Amy's big eyes looked as if she were ready to cry.

I touched the shoes. They felt a bit hard, but Amy would soon work them supple. "Hey, I'm glad for you. When do you move to the lower advanced class?"

"Friday," Amy said. "Tonight was my last night in my old class." She cradled her shoes against her stomach. "So I was wondering . . ." Her voice trailed off shyly.

It was strange to think that someone who got up onstage to dance could be shy in person, but Amy hardly spoke to anyone else but me and Leah and Thomas. "What is it?"

"Madame says that new shoes need old ribbons." Amy raised her shoes.

"And you want to have a set of my old ones?" I asked. At least part of me would be back with Madame. "I'd be honored. I'll give them to you tomorrow."

Amy smiled with relief, as if she had had doubts. "Thanks."

From her face, though, I could see there was something more she was dying to ask. "What else?" I asked.

Amy bit her lip. "Well, you know, if you were coming back, I wouldn't even bother you . . ."

"We're friends, Amy," I said. "What's mine is yours."

"Well, would it upset you if I did the Morning Butterfly at this year's recital?" She added guiltily, "It was Madame's idea, and of course I'd never be as good as you."

I felt like she had just punched me in the stomach. Up until now I had nursed a fantasy that I could return to the ballet school in time to dance as the Morning Butterfly in the next recital.

Suddenly I felt sad and angry, like someone who had just missed a train—except this train was my life.

Amy was scanning my face anxiously, while Leah eyed me sympathetically. "Just say the word," Amy said nobly, "and I won't do it."

Good old Amy. How could I hold a grudge against someone that sweet? I told myself I was being silly. The role wasn't my private property. It was time to be Amy's friend, not to feel sorry for myself.

I got up and started to stretch. "If you don't do it, who will?" I asked. "That awful Cynthia?"

"Her leaps are always better than mine," Amy said, trying to be nice.

"Leaps aren't everything, my dear." I grasped her

hand and tried to tug her to her feet. "Want me to show you the first part, or are you tired from class?"

Amy beamed her gratitude as she let me pull her to her feet. "I've still got all this energy that needs to be worked off. Is it okay, Leah?"

Leah beckoned from her open front door. "I wouldn't mind trying it out myself."

So we climbed directly to the rehearsal room, where we all did our stretching exercises. And then Leah put a CD into the player. The next moment I heard the "Dance of the Butterfly."

At one time, I thought that music was part of me, but I had deliberately avoided it since my last recital. Whenever it came on the tape, I fast forwarded it so I could begin the tape over again. Now, as I listened to the familiar notes, I just stood there, feeling leaden and dead.

"Show me," Amy said, and raised her arms. Leah lifted hers as well.

My body took over then. My arms began rising of their own volition, and my legs began to move. Watching me intently, Amy copied my movements a fraction behind the music. I had to adjust the steps for the room, but it felt good to be dancing again.

As I saw Amy imitate me, I felt a flicker of resentment, which I quickly stamped down. And though I was now dancing on the hardwood floor of Leah's room, my arms and legs felt no lighter than they had on the sidewalk. To my chagrin, I saw that there were now movements when Amy was smoother and better than I was. And that only made me feel worse inside.

Still, by the time we were finished, I had worked off my anger. I didn't feel any pleasure, though, just a great emptiness—and an aching in my feet.

Amy leaned her head to the side as she stared down at my legs. "You winced a couple of times. Did you pull a muscle?"

"It's just a little ache in the toes," I said. When I felt the sharp, stabbing pain, I did my best to control it.

Leah suppressed a yawn as she offered, "Would you like anything?"

My throat and mouth were so dry, I was dying for something cool and sweet. I would have liked nothing better than to have something to drink after our practice, but then I remembered that I had a Dove bar at home. It was my dessert for the week. I had saved it long enough. So, even though I was thirsty, I wasn't going to make my friends stay up any longer. "No, it's getting late. I'd better get home."

Unable to control her yawns anymore, Leah led us to the door. "You're sure?"

I gave her a quick hug. "I'm lucky to have friends like you."

As I headed home, all I could think of was that ice cream bar waiting for me. On the way, I dropped Amy off at her flat. "You really don't mind about my taking the role?" she asked.

For my friend's sake, I forced myself to smile. "It

couldn't go to a better dancer. I'm available any time you want to go over the rest."

Amy's eyes searched my face uncertainly, and then she hugged me impulsively. "Thanks, Robin."

After having been a good sport, I felt like I had earned my treat. So when I reached my own home, I bounded up the steps and headed straight for the kitchen.

Ian was in there already, eating an ice cream bar, while Grandmother sat with a paper napkin ready to wipe away any smears or spills. She had taught Ian enough Chinese so that they could hold short, simple conversations. Sometimes from the way they smiled at each other, it seemed as if they were sharing a secret joke about me.

"Good evening, *Paw-Paw*," I said.

"Good evening," she answered, keeping her eyes on Ian.

I went to the refrigerator and opened the freezer. The ice cube trays had fused to the metallic bottom. Piled on top were packages of frozen food and cans of frozen orange juice. I dug around for my ice cream bar. When I didn't find it right away, I began taking items out and stacking them on the kitchen table. When I had finally emptied out the entire freezer except for the ice trays, there was no sign of my ice cream bar.

With growing suspicion, I rounded on my heel. "Did you see my ice cream bar?" I asked.

Ian shrugged and went on eating.

"There were two ice cream bars in there yesterday. And I put my name on mine." I went to the plastic trash can and opened it, rummaging around until I found the cardboard container. Sure enough it had my name on it.

"That's mine," I said, displaying the container as evidence. "It was my special treat."

"I got hungry," he said.

"You had your own," I snapped.

"I finished it this afternoon." The little rat calmly went on nibbling at the bar. "Grandmother said it was all right."

"Big sisters need to share with little brothers." She patted him on the head to encourage him to go on eating. "Besides, I didn't think you wanted it. You just left it there."

First my role in *The Nutcracker*, and now my dessert. With the container in my hand, I went in search of Mom to complain. I found her going through some legal papers. Refusing to be put off any longer, I planted the container on top of the papers.

"Your son is a thief, and your mother tells him to steal. He ate my dessert for this week."

Mom blinked at the container as if she needed to focus her eyes. "What do you want me to do about it, Robin?"

That surprised me. "I want you to make him behave."

The chair creaked as Mom sat back. "He's a boy,

Robin. She was that way with my brothers too. Back in China, boys are everything."

"And what are we?" I asked.

Mom forced herself to smile. "We," she said softly, "are very understanding while my mother gets used to America."

"But Grandmother's a girl," I said. "Or was. She ought to know how I feel."

Mom shrugged. "It's Chinese tradition to put the boys before the girls. I'm sure she went through the same thing when she was your age."

Since Mom was basing her argument on Chinese custom, I thought I had her. "Well, if we were in China, who would take care of her? You or one of your brothers?"

Mom squirmed uncomfortably. "If we were there, Uncle Georgie or Uncle Eddy would, but we're here."

I clicked my tongue in exasperation. "Well, I don't think it's very fair by American customs. Uncle Georgie and Uncle Eddy were her special pets in China, and yet it's you that brought her over and it's you who's responsible for her."

Mom smiled sadly, as if she heard enough of that from Dad. "Whether we're talking American or Chinese, your grandmother's a survivor. Give her time and she'll learn how we do things here."

Furious, I left Mom. I had every intention of going to bed, but then I remembered the food I had taken from the freezer. The last thing I needed was to get scolded, so I went back to the scene of the crime.

I threw everything back into the freezer, not caring how much noise I made. It didn't seem to bother Grandmother and Ian in the slightest.

She sat on a kitchen chair with her head bent over close to his, whispering something to him in Chinese. As the two of them sat with their heads close together, I suddenly understood another reason for the difference in her treatment of me and him.

Though Ian and I both have the same brown eyes, his hair is black, while mine is brown like Dad's. In fact, everything about Ian looks more Chinese than me. It's me people stare at—as if I were a freak because I'm half American and half Chinese. I tell myself that it's because they're ignorant and they never learned manners, but it's hard when your own grandmother makes you feel that way.

I went to my room, sat down, and undid the drawstring of my special bag. I was so proud when Madame had said I was ready to use pointe shoes. When I lifted them out, the satin ribbons fluttered down around my wrists as if in a welcoming caress.

I almost cried as I slipped on the shoes. Then I got out the scissors and cut off the ribbons—wishing that they were a certain little monster's ears.

EIGHT

Ribbons

The next morning I was still feeling sorry for myself when I went into the kitchen. I was surprised to see Mom there, because she usually left early for the office. As soon as she saw me, she got up.

"What did I do now?" I asked defensively.

"I'd call that a guilty conscience." Coffee mug in hand, Mom went to the freezer and opened it. "There's your ice cream bar. And I've made it clear to Ian that I will revive the death penalty if he so much as looks at it. And it doesn't matter what your grandmother says."

I regarded it cautiously, expecting it to dematerialize at any moment. "Where did you get it?"

Mom shut the door. "From the store."

"You went out last night?" I asked. Mom was usually in bed by ten. She never did anything after sunset.

Mom took a last sip of coffee. "I had to pick up a couple of things."

I had been so busy wallowing in self-pity that I hadn't considered Mom. "It must have been near eleven." I felt guilty now. "I guess the ice cream bars could have waited."

Mom set the cup down in the sink. "Look, Robin, I know it's been a difficult period of adjustment."

I felt compelled to point out: "With her doing the ordering and us doing the adjusting."

"I know." Mom sighed. "It hasn't been easy for me either."

I took up the cup and began to wash it. It hadn't occurred to me before. "You went from being the boss to a slave, didn't you?"

"I can't wait till you grow up. Then I can come and live with you and your kids." Mom put an arm around my waist and gave me a hug. "Just do me a favor. Try to get along with your grandmother. Without her, you wouldn't exist."

The Debt again. I wondered when we would ever pay it off. I thought of what Mom had done last night and knew how important it was to her. "All right," I said. "I will."

At school, I gave Amy a box with the ribbons inside. I'd wrapped it up and stuck a lot of gold stars on it. Amy was so grateful that I was glad I had taken the extra time the night before to do that.

The rest of the day I thought about what Mom had said. Grandmother is a hero. She saved your mother and your uncles. I had to make more of an effort to know her and let her know me. She'll like you just as much as Ian once she gets to know you. And, I thought in a flash, the best way to know a person is to know what they love. For me, that was the ballet.

When I returned home and had done my homework, I got out the special bag from the box I had put it in. On the bottom of the box were the spare satin ribbons.

I could have asked Mom to help me attach the new ribbons to my shoes, but then I remembered that at one time Grandmother had supported her family by being a seamstress. Rather than just show the shoes to her, I would ask her for help. The more I thought about it, the more I figured it would be an even better way to introduce my chief love to her.

I got Mom's sewing kit, set my shoe and the ribbons on the lid, and padded barefoot into the living room; but I found that Grandmother had fallen asleep while watching television.

"*Paw-Paw*," I said, "can you help me?" I held up the silk ribbons, all ready to tell her about that special day when Madame Oblamov had "put me up" on my toes.

Grandmother reared back as if worms were dangling from my fingers rather than ribbons. "What for?"

I thought she might still be a little groggy. "These are special shoes for my ballet."

Holding up the shoes and the ribbons, I rose on

pointe to illustrate. "This is ballet." By now I felt a sharp pain whenever I did that, but I had learned to ignore it. Sometimes adhesive tape over my shoes helped.

Grandmother gazed in horror at my feet—as if I had turned into a vampire. "No," she said, and thumped a cane. "You mustn't do that."

Disappointed, I lowered the shoes and ribbons. "All right. I'll go into the kitchen. I didn't think I was disturbing you."

Thump. "You don't understand. You mustn't wear them at all."

Bewildered, I spread my arms out. "But how am I supposed to dance?"

"You mustn't dance. Look at what it's done to your feet already." When she looked back at the satin ribbons, it was with a hate and disgust that I had never seen before. She dropped one cane on the floor with a loud clatter and held out her hand. "Give them to me."

I clutched the shoes tightly against my stomach. "No. I need them for ballet."

Her eyes widened, as if she couldn't believe I was disobeying her. "Be good—like your brother."

That really set me off. Mom came running from the kitchen when she heard us both shouting. She immediately assumed it was my fault. "Stop yelling at your grandmother!"

By this point, I was in tears. "She's taken everything else. Now she wants to take away ballet."

"It's an awful thing to let her do." Grandmother jabbed a cane at my feet. "Look at her toes."

The adhesive tape had come loose so that my toes hooked downward again. Mom glanced down and then bent so she could examine them closer among the scraps of tape. "I guess I've been so busy that I haven't been keeping track of these things. When did your toes start to curl down, honey?"

I tried to flatten them out on the floor but I couldn't. "I don't know," I said.

Mom studied them from another angle. "Do they hurt?"

"No," I lied.

She shook her head. "I don't know. Maybe we shouldn't have been letting you dance unsupervised. I think you ought to see Dr. Brown." That was Leah's mother. A visit to Dr. Brown would be covered by my parents' medical plan.

Thump. "In the meantime," Grandmother ordered, "take her shoes away."

Mom sighed. "Yes, Mother."

I gaped at Mom in amazement. "Aren't you going to stand up for me?"

"Not now, honey," she whispered.

I hurt so much that I couldn't speak at first.

Mom got this trapped, exasperated look on her face.

"Don't make this any harder than it already is. All right?"

I just stared, helpless and angry.

"All right?" Mom repeated.

I knew I had to answer or Mom would mistake silence for insolence. "Don't do this to me, Mom," I pleaded.

"Please, honey." She worked the shoes and ribbons away from my stunned fingers. And I felt almost as if she had cut off my feet.

I grabbed Dad as soon as he got home. "Dad!" I called.

He stared up at me wearily from the bottom step. "Don't start on the lessons again, Robin. I had a hard day at the store."

The urgency made me start to descend the stairs to meet him. "But this can't wait." As he climbed the stairs heavily toward me, I told him what had happened.

"And your mother went along with it?" he asked doubtfully.

I backed up the last step to the floor of our flat. "*Paw-Paw*'s got her buffaloed."

"She's got all of us browbeaten," Dad muttered, more to himself than to me.

I clung to his arm. "So you'll help me get my shoes back and let me start my lessons?"

Dad looked guilty about that. "Some day," he said softly. "Just like I promised, lion."

Mom stepped out into the hallway. "I thought I heard you, Gil."

Indignantly Dad set down his knapsack. "What's this about Robin's shoes?"

Holding a sheaf of papers in her hand, Mom walked toward us. "I think Robin should rest from ballet."

Dad jabbed a finger at Mom. "Now look. I've put up with a lot from your family, but now I think you're going too far."

Mom slapped at his finger with her papers. "Let me finish. I want her to wait until Dr. Brown can check out her feet."

"My feet are fine," I insisted.

Mom jerked her head at me. "Show him, Robin."

"Take off your socks." Dad wriggled a finger at my feet.

"You're making a big thing out of nothing," I said. Raising one leg, I stood cranelike as I stripped off first one sock and then the other.

"See how the toes curl," Mom said.

Dad pointed at the little toe of my left foot. "She's got calluses the size of almonds. Does that hurt?" he asked, prodding one.

I forced myself to hide the pain and smile. "Of course not." I even jogged a few steps in place to show that I was in perfect health.

"I still think a doctor ought to see her," Mom said.

"I think so too." Dad straightened.

Mom poked him in the side with the legal brief. "You were pretty fast to blame my family."

Dad thrust his hands down toward the floor, as if he were shoving something down. "Cool it, will you? I've had an awful day."

"I haven't liked your attitude lately," Mom said, working her own sense of indignation up. "You're always making snide comments."

"But always in private." Dad jerked his head toward me. "Shall we continue this discussion later?"

Mom and Dad never used to talk like that. It was yet another sin to blame on Grandmother. With an effort, Mom brought herself back to the original topic. "All right, tonight."

Dad nodded and turned to me. "In the meantime, no dancing."

I felt all hollow inside; but by now I was beyond tears. I never expected my father to betray me like that. In a daze, I walked into the living room.

Grandmother looked at me from her chair. "This is for your own good," she said. She must have overheard everything.

I just stared at her. If she wanted war, then war it would be.

As it happened, Dr. Brown was out of town, so I couldn't see her for a couple of weeks. My mind imagined all sorts of terrible things. My legs would go as flabby as noodles in the meantime.

I was so angry that I decided that it was not enough to ignore my grandmother. That night I planned my campaign. I would always be polite so Grandmother would not have any ammunition against me; and I would always be the well-mannered host, but that would be all.

The next evening, I put my plan into motion. At dinner, I turned my chair around and ate with my plate on my lap so I would not have to look at her. Instead, I could stare at the wall.

"Sit right," Mom hissed.

"Yes, Mother," I said with formal politeness. So I faced back to the table, but I hunched over my plate.

"Sit up straight," Dad ordered.

"Yes, Father." I straightened up, but then I closed my eyes. Blindly I groped around with my chopsticks, knowing I was making a mess of things.

"Look at your food," Mom snapped.

"You told me to sit up straight," I said, pretending to look confused.

"Sit up straight and look at your food," Dad ordered.

"I wish you'd make up your mind." Picking up my chair, I turned it around to face the wall again.

As I picked up my plate, Mom threw down her napkin. "Young lady, if you can't eat properly, you won't eat at all."

"That's fine," I snapped.

"Let her eat in the living room," Grandmother said.

"Thank you," I said without looking her. Carrying my plate, I went into the living room to finish.

After that, I began to practice what I called the "polite cold shoulder." Finally one night as Ian and I lay in the dark in his bedroom, his voice floated down to me from his bed. "Why are you being so mean to Grandmother?"

"Because she's so mean to me," I said from my mattress.

"But you hurt her feelings," Ian protested.

"What do you think she did to me?" I demanded, feeling the righteousness of my cause.

I heard his bed creak as if he were changing positions. "The ballet made you smell," Ian insisted. "I'm glad she made you stop."

The topper came the next evening at dinner, when Grandmother and Ian announced that they were going to cook a meal together. Dad and Mom acted as if she had just given them a million dollars. "What can we get?" Dad asked eagerly.

Ian took out a list as long as his arm. "I helped Grandmother write up a list of ingredients."

Dad took it. "Look at this. It's got the Chinese too." He waved it in front of me to get my attention. "Do you think we can shop along Clement Street?"

I glanced at the list and went back to eating. "Probably."

"Want to come along?" he hinted.

"No, thank you."

"Oh, come on, Robin," Mom coaxed. "You know how much you enjoy going there."

I went on eating calmly. "I've got tons of homework. You yourself said that grades are important."

"Never mind," Dad said, giving up. "I'll take Ian along."

Dad bought a lot of things along Clement, and Mom got everything else—though to obtain one item she had to brave the traffic and drive into Chinatown itself, where it was so hard to park.

On the day of the big banquet, Grandmother and Ian were just like two bees buzzing all around. I could hear them in the kitchen, chopping and slicing up the ingredients.

Finally I heard the thumping of Grandmother's canes. I began gathering up my binder and textbooks immediately. I was just starting to get up when Grandmother came into the room.

"Hello," I said politely. Closing my eyes, I began to feel my way along.

"Robin, we need your help," Ian said from in front of me. "Grandmother shouldn't be on her feet, and she says I'm too young to cook."

I opened my eyelids enough to see the little toad blocking my way. "Sorry. I have to keep off my feet too. Wait until Mom or Dad comes home."

Slipping around him, I caught a glimpse of Grand-mother. When she didn't look very happy, I'm sorry to say that I began to gloat. Then, shutting my eyes, I found my way to the door and out of the room.

Because they couldn't precook some of the dishes ahead of time, dinner was very late that night. "Look at this," Dad said as he sat down. "It was worth the wait. Congratulations, *Paw-Paw* and Ian."

I, of course, kept looking at the wall. "What's that smell?" I asked.

"Dinner," Mom said, "and it's delicious."

"It stinks," I said. I had worn a loose sweatshirt. Unzipping it now, I took out the can of air freshener I had taken from the bathroom and hidden inside my clothes. "You know, Ian, it smells worse than when I used to dance and sweat."

I took off the lid, held up the can, and began to spray air freshener through the kitchen.

"You stop that this minute," Dad snapped.

I continued to spray, drawing fragrant lazy S's in the air. "But Ian's nose is so sensitive. I'm doing it for his own good."

Mom charged around the table Seizing my wrist, she yanked the can from my fingers and threw it across the kitchen. "Have you gone crazy?"

I pulled my arm free. "Yes," I said, fighting to keep from shouting. "Yes, I have." I rose slowly to my feet. "If you were good at something—something you loved—and someone took it away, wouldn't you go crazy too?"

Mom stared at me, baffled and hurt all at the same time. "But she's your grandmother."

"And she's taken away my ballet," I said, and left.

· N I N E ·

Bound Feet

For the next few days, things got more and more tense. I almost felt like I would lose the game if I saw Grandmother's face even once. A couple of times she called to me unhappily, but I used schoolwork as an excuse and escaped both times.

Ian stopped talking to me, but that was no big loss. He didn't understand yet that his silence was a blessing rather than a punishment. Mom, of course, looked as if I had tried to set Grandmother on fire, and Dad seemed afraid that I had gone crazy, so he treated me as if I were made of fragile crystal. At night, you could hear a low, angry murmuring coming from their room. Their "discussions" seemed less and less friendly, until it even began to spill over into the daytime, with frosty looks directed at each other.

I didn't care. In my opinion, they got what they had asked for.

Then one day when I came home from school, it was silent. If Grandmother had been around, the television would have been blasting away. So I thought she was gone. Mom went to work at the crack of dawn so she could get out early and pick up Ian. It wouldn't have surprised me if she had taken Ian and Grandmother out to see something—especially after the events of the last few days.

I felt relieved. The war hadn't been any too easy on my nerves either. I shrugged off my book bag, set it on the floor, and headed down the hallway to use the bathroom. When I twisted the knob, it wasn't locked, so I thought it was unoccupied.

I got a nasty jolt when I opened the door. Grandmother was sitting fully clothed on the edge of the bathtub. Her pants were rolled up to her knees, and she had her feet soaking in a pan of water.

"Don't you know how to knock?" she snapped, and reached for a towel.

"You usually lock the door," I said indignantly.

She tried to drop the towel over her feet, but she wasn't quick enough because I saw her bare feet for the first time. It was as if her feet were like taffy that someone had stretched out and twisted. They bent downward in a way that feet were not meant to, and her toes stuck up at odd angles, more like lumps than toes. I didn't think she had all ten either.

"What happened to your feet?" I whispered in shock.

Grandmother flapped a hand at the air for me to go. "None of your business. Now get out."

"But your poor feet," I said, feeling as if I should call 911.

"Out!" she shouted. She reached for another towel and threw it at me. "Out!" She was almost hysterical.

Despite everything I had done to her this week, I felt this was the most terrible thing. I had violated her deepest secret.

Hastily I backed out of the bathroom and shut the door behind me. However, I felt like I could still see her mangled feet. Even when I shut my eyes, I could still see them. Every tortured curve and twist of her feet had been chiseled into my memory.

Disgusted and horrified, I retreated to Ian's bedroom, where I sat on my mattress. I tried to forget by picking up a book, but I couldn't see the words. They kept becoming the dots that outlined my grandmother's feet.

I was still in the bedroom when Mom and Ian got home. I could hear Mom calling to Grandmother, and Ian thundered down through the hall as he ran to find her. I just sat there afraid to move.

She must have said something to Mom, though, because Mom knocked a moment later.

"What is it?" I asked.

Treating that as an invitation, Mom opened the door and came inside.

"I'd really like to be alone," I said.

Mom sat down on Ian's bed anyway. "Your grand-mother's very upset, Robin."

"I didn't mean to look," I said. "It was horrible." Even now when I closed my eyes, I could still see her twisted feet.

I opened my eyes when I felt Mom's hand on my shoulder. "She was so ashamed of them that she didn't like me to see them even when I was small."

"But what happened to them?" I wondered.

Mom's forehead furrowed, as if she were not sure how to explain things. "There was a time back in China when people thought women's feet had to be shaped a certain way to look beautiful."

"Beautiful?" I couldn't see how those hideous feet could be anybody's idea of beautiful.

Mom bit her lip as if she had stepped into water over her head. "People do odd things in the name of beauty. Some people flatten their foreheads. Others put wooden plugs in their lips. Even in America, you find women who wear shoes a couple of sizes too small just so they can appear to have little feet."

"This had to be a man's idea." I grimaced.

"Maybe, but for a while in China it was almost ev-erybody else's." Mom gestured to my feet. "When a girl was about five, her mother would gradually bend her toes under the sole of her foot."

"Ugh." Just thinking about it made my own feet ache. "Her own mother?"

Mom smiled apologetically. "Her mother and father thought it would make their little girl so beautiful that she could marry a rich man. They were still doing it in some of the back areas of China long after it was outlawed in the rest of the country."

"Is that what happened to Grandmother?" I was beginning to understand. When she had seen my curled toes and tape, she had leapt to the wrong conclusions.

"It's what I managed to piece together. As you've just seen, it's not anything she likes to talk about," Mom explained.

I shook my head. "There's nothing lovely about them."

"I know." Mom went on. "Feet were usually bound up in silk ribbons." Mom shoved some of the hair from my eyes. "Because the ribbons were a symbol of the old days, Grandmother undid them as soon as we were free in Hong Kong—even though they had kept back the pain."

I was even more puzzled now. "How did the ribbons do that?"

Mom began to brush my hair with quick, light strokes. "The ribbons kept the blood from circulating freely and bringing more feeling to her feet. Once the ribbons were gone, her feet ached. They probably still do."

I rubbed my own foot in sympathy. "But she doesn't complain."

"That's how tough she is," Mom said as she studied her handiwork.

Finally the truth dawned on me. "That's why she got so upset when she saw my feet."

Mom lowered the brush and nodded solemnly. "I think so. And maybe in her own misguided fashion, she didn't want you go to through what she did."

"Did you try and explain to her?" I asked.

Mom rested her elbows on her knees as she leaned forward. "Not yet. I wanted to wait for the doctor's report. She might respect that."

"Why are you so afraid of her?" I asked.

Mom smiled a little nervously. "It doesn't matter how old we get. She'll still be my mother, and I'll still be her little girl."

I felt a grief so deep that I could not understand it. "I've treated her so bad too."

"I wish I could have told you," Mom said.

"It's not her fault though," I argued.

Mom rocked up and down as she pressed her hands together. She reminded me of some broken toy. "I know. But it's beyond that. Don't mention it to Ian."

"Does Dad know?" I asked.

Mom gave her head a little shake. "Just you and me now."

It couldn't have been easy to shoulder the whole load by herself. I surged to my feet and went over and hugged her. Mom stayed huddled up like a small child. "I won't tell anyone," I promised. "And I won't give Grandmother a hard time."

Mom just smiled sadly and patted my hand. "Thank you." We were bound now by the same terrible secret. And I was determined that Mom would not have to bear that burden alone.

I guessed I had been wrong. Grandmother loved me in her own way. I was still trying to sort things out inside my head when I heard Grandmother and Ian outside in the hallway. Grandmother seemed to be hesitating, but Ian was insistent.

"It's my room," Ian said, and opened the door.

Grandmother stood there with her canes as if she were trapped, and then Ian was pulling her gently inside.

I didn't turn away this time, but she refused to look at me—as if I had become tainted by her secret.

"I want a story," Ian said.

Grandmother wouldn't meet my eyes. "Would you read to him? I can't."

"Do you need a pair of reading glasses?" I asked.

Grandmother shook her head. "I can't read English."

"But you speak it so well," I said, getting up to help her.

She made her own way through the maze of boxes and over my mattress. "That's what I needed for employment," she said, sitting down. She looked as if she didn't relish the idea any more than I did.

Wanting to get this awkward moment over, I motioned to Ian. "All right. I'll read you one story."

Naturally Ian chose the fattest book he could, which was my old collection of fairy tales by Hans Christian Andersen. Years of reading had cracked the spine, so that it fell open automatically in his hands to my favorite story when I was small. It was the original story of "The Little Mermaid"—not the cartoon. The picture illustrating the tale showed her posed like a ballerina in the middle of the throne room.

When I was young, I had misinterpreted the picture. Because she stood like a ballerina, I thought she moved like one too. It seemed like such a marvelous thing to have a magical spell that could change you into a ballerina. Even at that age, I would have paid the price she had—though each step caused her pain. When my parents did not want to read the whole story to me, I would get them to read me the page about her transformation.

"This one," Ian said, and pointed to the picture of the Little Mermaid.

While he and Grandmother sat on Ian's bed, I began to read. But when I got to the part where the Little Mermaid can walk on land, I stopped.

Ian was impatient. "Come on. Read," he ordered, patting the page.

"After that," I went on, "each step hurt her, as if she were walking on knives." I couldn't help looking up at Grandmother, wanting to let her know that I now understood.

For once she didn't try to avoid me or push me away. Instead, she was the one who tapped the page. "Go on. Tell me more about the mermaid."

So I went on reading to the very end, where the mermaid is changed into the foam on the sea. "That's a dumb ending," Ian said. "Who wants to be pollution?"

"Sea foam isn't pollution. It's just bubbles," I explained. "The important thing was she wanted to walk, even though it hurt."

"I would rather have gone on swimming," Ian insisted.

"But maybe she wanted to see new places and people by going on the land," Grandmother said softly. "If she had kept her tail, the land people would have thought she was odd. They might have even made fun of her."

When she glanced at her own feet, I thought she might be talking about herself—so I seized my chance. "My satin ribbons aren't like your old silk ones. I use them to tie my shoes on." Setting the book down, I hurriedly got out a picture that Thomas had taken of me. "Look."

Ian sat bored, but Grandmother studied the photo.

Almost shyly her fingertip stroked the ribbons in the picture. "You must think it's a big joke. Your grandmother is so old-fashioned."

"But you're modern. Mom says you go through a lot to be modern. You're a lot braver than the Little Mermaid." I let my eyes glance down meaningfully at her feet, and then I raised them again.

She stared at me for a long while. Suddenly she lifted a hand, and I flinched, thinking she was going to hit me; but she got such a sad look on her face that I stopped drawing back. Instead, I made myself sit still.

Grandmother smiled as she completed the caress, brushing the hair from my eyes. "So you don't think I'm funny?"

It was the first time I had seen any uncertainty in her, and it made me begin to like her. I sat down beside her. She had a sweet, musky smell that was a mixture of incense and the soap she used. "I think you're very brave."

"Brave about what?" Ian asked as he tried to puzzle out our secret code.

"Brave to put up with you, squirt," I said to him, and then turned back to Grandmother.

She took my hand and squeezed it clumsily. "I was so scared you'd laugh at me. A whole ocean and a new country, but that was my biggest fear."

I laced my fingers through hers. "What did I do to make you think that?"

She squeezed my hand. "You have so much here. You reminded me of the rich girls back home in China. They used to make fun of me for crying." She glanced down at her feet, as if she meant when her feet were bound.

"And Ian didn't scare you?" I asked, feeling hurt.

"He's young. He can't hide the way he feels," Grandmother explained.

"I can so," Ian said, feeling as if he had to defend himself, though he didn't know why.

Remembering what Mom had said about herself and her brothers, I thought to myself, *And he was a boy.*

With her free arm, Grandmother drew him against her other side. "You'll turn into a stranger when you grow up. You all do. And then I'll learn to get scared of you too."

And I began to suspect why Grandmother had been so distant to me at first. She thought I would mock her so she had been careful to keep me away so I could not hurt her even more. And then I had started my war with her—which had only reinforced her first fears.

Suddenly I found myself wanting to hug her myself. So I did. Though she was stiff at first, she gradually softened in my arms.

"I'm sorry for what happened," I said in a low voice. "Can we start over?"

"Yes, yes," she whispered fiercely.

I felt something on my cheek and realized she was crying, and then I began crying too.

"So much to learn," she said, and began hugging me back. "So much to learn."

The Rescue

Now that I felt the tie between Grandmother and me, I just couldn't ask about lessons. I would wait for the doctor's appointment, and then we would see.

Dad was surprised when I sat with my chair facing the table. Without calling specific attention to it, he beamed. "Well, isn't this a happy scene," he said, relieved, and passed a bowl of black bean chicken to me.

I didn't want to call any more attention to it, so I took the chicken. "Not when you've seen Ian's report card." It was a very simple report card for kindergarten, with stars rather than grades.

Ian scowled at me. "Fink."

I made a face back. "Know what you get when you cross a skunk and a fink?" I answered my own question immediately, "You get a skink, and that's you."

"You spoke too soon," Mom said calmly as she took the dish from me. "Next time wait awhile before you talk."

Later, when we had settled in the living room, Mom was going to put on a Chinese movie she had rented from Clement Street, but Dad stopped her.

"Have you seen this, *Paw-Paw?*" he asked. Squatting, he fished around through the videotapes in the cabinet with the VCR. "What's that doing in here?" he muttered, and pulled out a *Wolf Warriors* movie— the latest fad in Ian's circle. When he pulled the tape from the box, I saw it was the videotape he had made of the school recital.

"Don't show that," I coaxed, wishing desperately that I had erased it.

Dad looked over his shoulder and winked. "You leave this to me."

However, I wasn't sure I could watch it without crying. "I'd rather not."

Mom's view was blocked by Dad's body, so she was twisting around to catch sight of it. "Gil, don't. You'll upset mother."

Dad, however, fended her off. "Assuming Dr. Brown gives her okay, she'll have to deal with it."

"Not now, Gil," Mom warned in a low, annoyed voice. It reminded me of the angry murmurings I heard nightly from their room. As much as I wanted to begin my lessons, it made me feel bad to think that they might be the root of the friction between Mom and Dad. I just hoped that now that I was trying to make peace with Grandmother, they could patch things up between themselves as well.

Dad was a gentle man, so when he lost his temper, it was always a shock. "Yes, right now!" he barked, and shoved the tape into the VCR. "My mother wanted to see it. It's part of the grandmotherly code. So yours should too."

"What is it?" Grandmother asked.

"Robin's last ballet recital." Dad turned the television to channel 3.

I looked from Grandmother to Mother. Mom was looking mad now. I started to get up. "Please, Dad."

In his own clumsy way, he wanted to help me. I couldn't clue him in to what had happened, because I had promised Mom not to speak about my discovery.

"Stop it, Gil," Mom said, and tried to reach over him to eject the tape.

Dad raised his shoulder and held Mom back. "It's time to think about someone else for a change." Before Mom could make another try to stop him, he punched the play button. Figures in bright costumes began to drift across the stage. In the case of some of the beginners, it was more like stumble.

"I've heard about ballet." Grandmother shifted in her chair to watch from a better angle. "But this is the first I've seen. I want to watch."

Mom slapped her hands helplessly against her side. And I felt like I was in a car heading for the river when the bridge was out. And all I could do was watch the disaster coming.

"There she is." Dad pointed proudly at the screen where I appeared.

Hearing the music made me ache to dance; but I forced myself to say, "It's silly."

Grandmother leaned forward, curious. A slow smile spread across her face. "How lovely."

I thought Grandmother was just saying grandmotherly things. It's strange to see yourself on television. No matter how many videotapes of me I've watched, I've never gotten used to it. Even though it had been less than a year ago, I felt like the girl on the screen was a stranger. Younger, shorter, and much, much too self-centered.

However, she also looked so much happier. She thought she would have ballet forever. No one had asked her for any real sacrifices yet. And she was certainly ignorant of the terrible things people could do to one another—like mothers binding their babies' feet. She was just . . . innocent.

And as I looked at the little auditorium stage, I couldn't help thinking that the production seemed terribly amateurish. The backdrops were crude, and a lot of the students just wanted to wear something pretty and bounce around to the music. And yet I would have matched Madame against any teacher at the San Francisco Ballet School. Who knows where I could have gone after she had finished training me. But that was all silly speculation now.

"She was the best onstage," Dad said proudly. "Listen to the applause."

Grandmother turned to me. "Is that why you like to dance?"

That wasn't what made me hungry inside. Since that first day when Grandmother had come, I had thought over several times what I once tried to explain to Dad. "It's not the clapping—though it's nice. It's . . ." I remembered again how it had been to move into the light. "You feel part of something that's bigger than you."

Grandmother turned back to Dad. "Show me again."

Picking up the remote control, Dad froze the action and then backed up. "Look at that, will you?" He set the tape into advance at a slow speed so he could trace the action with his fingers.

While Dad explained the dance to Grandmother, Grandmother nodded her head wistfully. "You're so beautiful. But some terrible things are done in the name of beauty." I know she was thinking of her own feet.

I couldn't be selfish after what had happened to her. "A lot of things," I said, trying to sympathize with her.

Grandmother stared at the screen thoughtfully. "Your eyes are looking elsewhere. Stop the tape." Dad froze me in mid-jeté. "There, what do you see?"

I sat upon my heels, squeezing my feet beneath me.

"Do you know how you feel when you hear your favorite song!"

Grandmother thought for a moment. "Something so sweet it just makes you ache inside?"

And in that instant I understood, and so did she. "Well, that's what it's like. Except you *are* the song."

Suddenly I felt little needles sting the corners of my eyes. Here I was, feeling sorry for myself because I had lost ballet. But my grandmother had lost so much more. She would never be able to dance at all. I didn't know whom to mourn for more: myself or my grandmother. It made me feel all torn up inside.

I started to get up to leave, but it was already too late. The tears coursed down my cheeks. Hastily I raised a sleeve to wipe them, but then Ian pointed at me. "Robin's crying."

"I just thought of one of your awful jokes," I said, trying to use humor to draw attention away from me. "They always make me cry."

Mom was really getting angry now. "Gil, turn it off."

Dad stood there stubbornly as I drifted across the screen in slow motion in jerky twitches. "But I wanted Grandmother to see how important ballet is to Robin."

"She knows," Mom said, and pointed. Grandmother was watching me rather than the television. "So stop the tape."

"But look at what this dancing does to your feet." Grandmother gestured to her own feet in distress. "When will it stop? When your feet are almost useless?"

"No, they won't be . . ." My voice trailed off. I almost said, "like yours."

It all seemed so hopeless because I was no nearer to beginning classes again.

"That bad?" Grandmother finished for me.

I told myself to stop thinking only of myself. I tried to use my fingers to wipe away the tears, but only wound up smearing them across my cheeks. "I'm sorry."

"Never show that tape again, Gil," Mom ordered. From the expression on her face, I knew there was going to be another angry discussion that night.

It was as if a bomb had gone off in the room. I sat like a shell-shocked survivor. Things seemed to be going from bad to worse between Mom and Dad. And it was all my fault.

ELEVEN

Language Lessons

The next day was a half day at school, so I came home early. I thought maybe if I could make things better between Grandmother and me, things would get better between Dad and Mom.

"It's time you learned about American soap operas," I told her.

"They're interesting?" she asked cautiously.

"Very," I assured her. Since I wasn't dancing, I decided to indulge myself and have one of my favorite snacks. "I even brought a bag of potato chips to split."

"I don't like them." Grandmother waved her hand in front of her nose as if there were a foul odor. "They smell too fishy."

Perplexed, I pulled the bag from the paper sack. "How do these smell fishy? These are onion-flavored."

It was Grandmother's turn to be puzzled. "Where's the fish?"

"What's fish got to do with chips?" I asked, and ripped open the bag. It had been months since I had last been wicked about my favorite food.

When I took out a chip, she pointed at it, annoyed. "That's not a chip. That's a crisp."

"Maybe to the English, who don't know any better." I dangled the chip before her. "But you're here now."

"I love crisps," she said as she reached for it.

I snatched it back. "Uh-uh. Chips."

"All right, chips," she snapped impatiently, and grabbed it as soon as it was close enough. "I love chips," she said as she crammed it into her mouth. "These are very good chips," she said, emphasizing the last word again.

"I knew it. It must be in the genes," I said, settling down to snack with her.

Today's episode was a good one, with the leading lady being buried alive. Grandmother waved her hand in frustration. "You shouldn't have made me watch it if it's going to end."

She was so irritated that I knew she was hooked. That must have been genetic too. "Don't worry. They'll bring her back. Or if this character's dead, she'll come back as her twin." I paused and scratched my head because I vaguely remembered she had already come back as her own double. "Or maybe as her triplet."

Grandmother turned the bag upside down and

placed her palm beneath. When only crumbs fell out, she grumbled, "Next time get two bags of criops."

"Chips," I corrected her.

"Chips," she said, and then made a face at me. It was so unexpected that I laughed.

During commercials, she gave me a quick English lesson. Mom had been over here so long that she had picked up most of the Americanisms, so I knew a lift was an elevator. But I didn't know that a chip to the English was a thick french fry and was usually served with fish. And I hadn't realized that the bonnet of the car was our hood.

"And what's the Chinese?" I asked, and then practiced what she told me.

As I repeated the words, she idly extended a hand and let her fingers stroke a strand of my hair. "So pretty," she said.

I sat still. "You don't think I look funny?"

"No more than me," she said, as if she was certain now that I would never mock her.

There was so much to know about each other that we chatted away as if we both felt we had already lost too much time. We were still talking when Mom and Ian came home. And when Dad eventually showed up, we were almost giddy.

"I think it's time to change my hair," Grandmother announced at dinner.

"Fine," Mom said. "I'll make an appointment at my beauty parlor."

"No, I want to go to Robin's friend." Grandmother pointed at me and winked. "I want spikes like I see on television." She raised a strand of her own hair in illustration.

I rested my chin on my hand. "I think purple would be nice."

"Pink, please," Grandmother said with great dignity.

Mom glanced back and forth between us as if she were trying to decide if we were serious or not. She wound up not taking any chances. "You are not doing anything to my mother," she said to me, and then turned to Grandmother. "And you are not doing anything to your head that I would not do to mine."

Grandmother muttered something in Chinese. Mom leaned her head to the side. "I beg your pardon."

"It's new street slang from Hong Kong," I told Mom.

"And how do you know?" Mom demanded.

"I told her," Grandmother said.

Mom was looking annoyed and bewildered at the same time. "And what does it mean?"

"We aren't telling you." Grandmother laughed, and I joined in.

Mom stiffened resentfully, but after a moment she relaxed and a deadly smile crossed her face as she regarded me. "I'm going to remember this when you have children. And I will have my revenge."

Grandmother tapped her wrist. "Don't say that, or she might not have them for a long, long time."

Things went so well that I brought Leah, Amy, and Thomas over on Saturday, and they were more than happy to accept an invitation on short notice. "I've been curious about the mystery woman," Thomas confessed.

"She's full of her mystery, all right," I said, stopping by a supermarket.

Leah was shocked when she saw me pick up two bags of chips. "That's fifty pounds right there."

"Grandmother will eat most of them." I started to take a couple of steps toward the counter, and then said, "Oh, what the heck," and went back and grabbed a third.

I noticed, though, that even Leah indulged in three chips and swilled down a regular, sugar-filled Coke. I thought Grandmother might be shy, but she recognized Thomas, Leah, and Amy from the videotape.

"You're the dancers," she said with delight. "I saw you on television." It made them semicelebrities in her eyes, and my three friends were pleased.

After chatting for a while, we wound up putting in the recital tape again. Leah, Thomas, and Amy laughed and elbowed one another, pointing out each other's mistakes to Grandmother. And Grandmother was an appreciative audience.

However, when it came time for my solo, everyone

grew serious. Grandmother turned to me. "We can stop it."

Though it still hurt inside, it was not as bad as the other day. "If you're getting bored."

"No," she said. "I would rather watch it. You're so graceful."

Thomas had noted her canes when he had first come in, but with uncharacteristic tact he had refrained from questioning her. "Did you ever dance, *Paw-Paw?*" He, Leah, and Amy had all taken to calling her that.

I held my breath, thinking that Grandmother might be sensitive on the subject, but she surprised me. "Oh, but I can."

And as we watched, she raised her canes, moving them in arabesques and spirals with elegant, graceful wrists. "These are my legs."

It was too whimsical to be grotesque. Grandmother was smiling all the while, as if she were sharing a private joke with us. None of us watched the television, and when the music was done, she lowered her canes. "I used to do that at home." She added shyly, "When you're by yourself, you do funny things."

I gave her a hug. "Well, you're not alone anymore."

TWELVE

Sunday in the Park
with Grandmother

It was Grandmother's idea to go for a walk on Sunday with just Ian and me. "You stay home," she told Mom. "Baby-sit your husband for a change." She could hear them quarreling as well as I could.

"Are you sure you're up to it?" Mom asked doubtfully.

"Yes, I'm sure." Grandmother was already rising from her chair with my help. "You're so nervous all the time, you make me nervous too."

Despite Grandmother's words, it wasn't possible to make a clean escape from Mom. She hovered over us as we got dressed, and checked us to make sure we had enough layers of clothing for a crisp fall day.

Even after we had passed inspection, she followed us down the steps with various instructions and warnings As we fled through the front door, Mom cautioned us one last time: "And don't forget to look both ways before crossing the street."

Grandmother, safely buttressed on either side by Ian and me, looked over her shoulder. "I know how to cross a street. I taught you. Remember? And Hong Kong traffic is a lot worse."

The street sloped gently downward toward the park, where the trees stood bright and thick as one of Grandmother's knit sweaters—and it looked just as comfortable and inviting. As we started down the sidewalk, Grandmother whispered to me, "Look behind us. Is your mother there?"

When I did, I saw Mom had followed us out onto the sidewalk. "You're right," I said.

Grandmother smiled in vindication. "Tell her to go back inside. It's cold, and she doesn't have a sweater."

It was sweet to have to remind Mom for a change. When I had told her, she dipped her head in embarrassment and scooted back inside.

It was a cool but sunny morning, and the park was full of people. On Sundays, automobile traffic was stopped in this part of the park, so the main drive was full of bicycles and skaters dressed in neon-colored spandex shorts and tops.

"Let's rest for a moment and watch," Grandmother said, nodding to a nearby bench.

My own feet were starting to hurt a little the way they always seemed to now, so I was grateful. After we had sat down, Grandmother waved her cane to indicate the stream of human-powered traffic. "It looks like a bag of rags just blew up," she said. "All those bright pieces flying all around." Her cane indicated chaotic swirls.

I had seen the scene so many times that I had begun to take it for granted. It was nice to see it through someone else's eyes. I was hunting for a poetic image of my own when Ian brought us to reality.

"I want to skate," he said. "We can rent them outside the park." On the street bordering the north side of the park, we had passed by a man renting rollerblades from the back of his station wagon.

"There's no way Mom would let you on skates without pads and a helmet," I said.

Grandmother nudged Ian. "Sometime we'll rent them together." And she kicked her feet up and down.

"Not unless I can tie leashes to you both," I teased.

It was a very nice morning to be in the park. There were people determined to take advantage of the sun. Even though it was still cool, they were sitting on the grass, trying to get a tan as they read the Sunday paper.

We stopped by one section where a kind of courtyard with posts barred entrance from the street. To the tunes from a huge boom box, various skaters tried to dance or even perform acrobatic stunts. We left shortly because Grandmother was afraid we'd hurt our ears. I didn't want to tell her how loud Amy and I listened to music.

At another intersection we waited as skaters rolled down a slalom course that had been set up with paper cups on a hill. When there was a break, we headed across. I kept looking up the hill and remembering Mom's last warning. To protect Grandmother, I was ready to block the next human missile. Fortunately, we made it to the other side.

After another rest, we went to the Conservatory of Flowers, which gleamed bright as a frosted ice cream cake. Dad said it was a scaled-down version of the Crystal Palace, which had been famous in the last century. We strolled through the flower beds, where the plants had been arranged to make pictures. Inside there were all sorts of exotic plants, so the air was hot and muggy.

Grandmother fanned herself, but she seemed happy. "This is more like it," she said.

After another rest among the flowers, we headed over to the bandshell. It was a sunken oval, with the museum to the north and the Academy of Sciences to the south.

Ian immediately wanted ice cream from the truck parked on one edge, so Grandmother treated us, counting out the amount as she plunked down each strange American coin. Then we sat down on one of the benches among the pigeons and the humans to listen to the uniformed musicians play.

"What else would you like to see?" I whispered to Grandmother. "The Academy has an aquarium and all sorts of other things. And then there's the Japanese tea garden. And beyond that is the botanical gardens." I waved my hand in their directions.

A bit of melted vanilla coursed down toward her hand, but her tongue intercepted the ice cream adroitly. "We'll see it some other Sunday. I think it's time to go back, before your mother gets too worried and calls the police."

I finished up my ice cream. "Was she always so serious? What about when she was a little girl?"

Grandmother glanced around as if to make sure that Mother was not lurking somewhere. "Always. She was a regular little old lady when she was five."

"I can imagine." I grinned.

"Did she ever have any fun?" Ian wondered.

"I don't think so," Grandmother said. She licked the remnants of her ice cream bar. When she pulled out the stick, it was clean. She contemplated the stick for a moment. "Maybe that's my fault. I was always too busy working. So your mother had to take care of Edward and Georgie. Maybe she had to grow up too fast."

"All she wants to do is work," Ian frowned.

She gave the stick one last lingering lick. "We'll change that."

I pressed my empty stick against hers. "All for one."

Ian used his clean stick as a sword, and then joined us. "And one for all," he said.

Though Grandmother seemed puzzled by the reference to *The Three Musketeers*, she added, "Quite."

As we headed out of the park, I began to think we had overdone it. Grandmother needed more frequent rests, and my feet were hurting so much that I almost limped. Even Ian was tired. As the sun grew hotter, he had taken off his sweatshirt, but I made him tie the arms around his waist so he wouldn't lose it.

However, on the edge of the park, Grandmother perked up immediately. "What's that?" she asked, pointing toward a sign painted on brightly colored cardboard.

"A garage sale," I read for her.

"What's that?"

"People sell things they don't want," I said.

"Cheap?" she asked.

"Sometimes," I said.

The thought of a bargain was the perfect tonic for Grandmother. "Let's go," she said, pulling me along.

My own feet were aching, so I was looking forward to resting at home. "I thought you were tired."

"Later," Grandmother said. It was like trying to hold on to a tank in a wool sweater. There was no stopping her.

The sale was on a street where all the houses had been built at the same time—three-story boxes jammed against each other. Without front lawns, they all crowded right against the sidewalk.

We didn't need to remember the address because there was such a big crowd in front of the house giving the sale. And there were cars and vans double- and even triple-parked outside.

As sales went, I didn't think much of it. But then I never cared for garage sales. They always made me feel like I was intruding in someone's life, and they usually made me sad because there would be someone's former treasures now abandoned—even old family photos. And I never liked to buy used clothes because they always seemed to be crawling with invisible germs from the previous owner.

This one wasn't any different. There were the usual old appliances people didn't want. Piles of *National Geographic* magazines. Old 78 albums. Chipped, rejected sticks of furniture.

However, that didn't stop people from crowding in—Grandmother included. I was afraid that she would get knocked over, so I tried to stop her.

Her eyes were gleaming with the vistas before her—like a pirate in front of the viceroy's treasure chamber. "Don't be silly. This is easy compared to shopping in Hong Kong," and she hobbled right into the garage.

"Don't lose sight of her," I grunted to Ian, and tried to squeeze after her.

I can't really say who were worse. I think it was a toss-up between the little old Chinese ladies and the little old Russian ladies; but after I got hit by their elbows several times, it made me wish that I'd worn a flak jacket. And I would have gotten between them and a bargain as I would have stepped between a starving dog and a bone.

"Hey! That belongs to me," I heard Ian shout shrilly behind me.

I turned to see an indignant lady with his sweatshirt in her hand. "It was on the floor."

The knot holding the sweatshirt's arms around his waist must have come undone. "That's mine." Ian grabbed one arm.

I felt like a salmon swimming upstream, but I forced my way through the crowd over to them. "Hey, lady, that's his," I said.

"I don't see his name on it," the bargain-hunter insisted.

They might have pulled it in half if a white-haired lady in a pink blouse hadn't come over. She had on an embroidered apron with pockets that jingled with change. "What's going on?" she demanded.

"She's trying to steal my sweatshirt," Ian puffed.

The bargain-hunter, however, tried to ignore Ian and appeal directly to the lady in the apron. "I don't see any price on this."

"That proves it's my brother's," I said.

The lady in the apron examined it. "I don't recognize it," she said uncertainly. "But a bunch of us are giving this sale so I'm not sure."

"It fell right from this table." The bargain-hunter indicated a metal folding table. At one time, there may have been neatly folded piles of children's clothes, but it was all one jumble now.

I pointed at the pocket. "It's got stains from the ice cream we just had."

The lady released the sweatshirt. "I don't want it anyway if it's dirty." She sniffed, and then crammed herself into a mob by a different table.

I didn't give the lady in the apron any choice as I helped Ian into his sweatshirt. "Let's find Grandmother and get out of here."

Ian nodded his head enthusiastically. "Yeah, before somebody buys us."

"Ladies, ladies," I heard the lady in the apron saying.

"I saw this first," Grandmother insisted.

Grabbing Ian's hand tightly, I wedged into the crowd to find Grandmother supporting herself with one cane. Somehow she had reversed the other cane so she could hold it from the bottom while she used the hook part to snag a transparent bag of yarn.

"Grandmother, let go," I said.

However, she was heavily infected with garage-sale fever. "This is mine. I was looking at it."

"How do I know that?" the other woman demanded. "Anyway, you hadn't touched it, and I did. The first one to grab it gets it. It is a rule of every garage sale."

I looked past the cane toward Grandmother's opponent. "Madame?" I asked in a hushed voice.

THIRTEEN

Madame

Madame Oblamov's stern face suddenly creased into a smile. "Robin? How have you been all this time?" In her other hand she had a pink plastic bag with oranges. It was the first hint I had that Madame had to eat like the rest of us mere mortals.

"You know my granddaughter?" Grandmother asked, though she did not relinquish her claim.

Neither did Madame Oblamov as she nodded her head warily. "Ah, you are the grandmother." She sized up Grandmother intently, her eyes lingering on the canes.

Grandmother spread her feet for better balance. "Who are you?"

"Madame Oblamov is my ballet teacher," I explained, and formally introduced them.

"On videotape, I have seen my granddaughter dance," Grandmother said to Madame. "You are a very good teacher."

Madame's stiff head bent ever so slightly toward Grandmother in acknowledgment of the compliment. "There are schools that may be bigger, but not better. When I am finished with my students, they can go anywhere."

In a way, Grandmother and Madame were a lot alike: They both were strong, stubborn, independent women. In fact, I could have seen Madame trudging in crippled feet across a continent with her children in tow. Since both seemed perfectly ready to stand there all day rather than surrender their bargain, I suggested, "There's plenty of yarn. Why don't you divide it between yourselves?"

They studied each other as they considered the proposal. Finally, Madame loosened up even more and dipped her head cautiously. "She makes sense."

"Of course," Grandmother said, and couldn't resist adding, "She gets it from me."

I think either one of them would have been formidable in a bargain, but the sales lady was no match for them as a pair. Madame pointed out flaws in the yarn that she had been so eager to buy a moment ago. And what flaws she didn't find, Grandmother did. By the time they were finished, the lady let it go for a dollar.

"Let's go outside and split the yarn," I said after they had paid her.

Madame clicked her purse shut. "Not till we've looked at everything."

Grandmother was already eyeing the other tables

with all the intensity of a hawk inspecting a hapless flock of hens. "That looks interesting," she said, nodding. Eagerly she shifted a cane from her right hand into her left and checked her coat pocket. "But I don't have any money left."

Madame regarded Grandmother's canes. "Don't your legs hurt?"

Grandmother shifted uneasily on her canes as if she disliked having attention called to her legs and feet. "It's nothing that I'm not used to."

"So." Madame nodded approvingly. Her estimation of Grandmother went up another notch. "Once in *Swan Lake*, I landed the wrong way. My foot started hurting but I finished. Later, when they X-rayed my foot, they found it was broken in three places."

Grandmother smiled as if she had found a kindred spirit—someone just as tough as she was. "Then you understand. When you have something to do, you finish it no matter what."

Madame grinned back at Grandmother, acknowledging the bond. "Just so."

Grandmother swung up a cane and jabbed it toward the garage. "So go back inside."

However, Madame threw her arm around Grandmother's shoulder. "Let me loan you the money and you can pay me back."

Grandmother was surprised and pleased. "You don't know me."

Madame was hard as steel on the outside, but if you could get beneath the armor plating, she could be as soft as butter. "You are Robin's grandmother. That is recommendation enough," Madame assured her partner-in-looting.

Madame's expansive warmth made Grandmother almost shy. "Thank you," she said. Licking her lips, she studied the garage and then turned to Ian. "Do you see that shawl?"

Ian stood on tiptoe to see better. "The blue one?"

Grandmother crouched so her mouth was at the level of his ear. "That's the one. Get it for me."

Ian dubiously eyed the surging elbows. "It's kind of crowded."

On the other side, Madame also squatted down so she could speak to him better. "I saw a table of toys in the corner," she coaxed slyly. "After we are done, you can pick one."

Ian let go of my hand as if it were suddenly greased. "Okay."

As Ian plunged back into the struggle, I glanced indignantly at first Madame and then Grandmother. "Aren't you two ashamed—letting Ian risk his neck like that to do your dirty work?"

Grandmother straightened up. "No," she said.

Madame stood up at the same time. "Coming?"

I folded my arms and grumbled, "Well, I'm finished."

"Good," Madame grunted. "You can watch these." And she thrust her oranges and the yarn into my hands.

I managed to make it out to the sidewalk without breaking any ribs. Every now and then, when the crowd parted momentarily, I could see Grandmother and Madame inside the garage. They were still using Ian to fetch for them. He was so small and agile he could wiggle into anywhere to get whatever they wanted. I had once read about hunters in Europe who used ferrets to go into difficult places for them.

They each came out with a shopping bag full of what was essentially somebody else's junk but which was now their own personal treasures. And once they were safely out of the battlefield, they divided the yarn, each taking a turn to pick out a ball. Fortunately, there was an even number.

They split up their booty with a kind of camaraderie now—like veterans who had just been through a battle. I had been dragged into enough garage sales by Mom that I knew the proper post-shopping rituals.

Naturally they had to admire each other's hard-won prizes in a more leisurely way. (Why Grandmother wanted a framed photo of somebody called Sonny Tufts eluded me—even if it was autographed.)

When they were finished enjoying each other's bargains, Grandmother indicated her bag. "And all that for only seven dollars."

"Ha!" Madame triumphantly indicated her bag. "Only five."

Grandmother tried to defend her reputation. "I had to buy the dinosaurs for Ian."

Ian was too absorbed in playing with his new toys to pay attention to any of us.

Now that the traditional rituals had been performed and the spirits of shopping appeased, I thought it was safe to ask, "Grandmother, aren't you tired?" My own feet had begun to hurt, so I had sat down on the sidewalk.

"I am a little," Grandmother admitted grudgingly.

Madame was instantly solicitous for her companion-in-plundering. "Then you must rest. And afterwards, we will take you home."

She talked the lady in the apron into letting Grandmother sit in a chair until it was sold. Then she turned and gave me a big hug. "I have missed you, Robin. Have you been practicing your ballet?"

I decided not to tell her about my problems. "Faithfully."

"Too much," Grandmother grunted.

Madame was suddenly on her guard, as she was whenever ballet was involved. "Your granddaughter has a great talent," Madame explained firmly but politely.

"Thank you," Grandmother said with equal manners, "but tell her not to work so hard."

From the way Madame arched her eyebrows, you would have thought Grandmother had accused her of dynamiting a bank. "We mustn't waste her ability."

"Madame, please," I begged, trying to head off a confrontation.

That was like trying to stop a runaway truck. Madame looked over my head, straight at Grandmother. "Dance is like a language. And the steps are like words. She has to practice." Madame struggled to find the right words. "If your granddaughter was a singer, would you tape her mouth shut? Would you tell a painter she could not use paint? Or a poet she could not use words?"

Grandmother stiffened, insulted by Madame. "Beauty is not everything."

"Beauty is special. It is like a pool of light. It cools. It warms." Madame hugged herself in illustration. "It makes you sad." She used her fingers to pantomime tears. "It makes you happy. It makes you alive. But not everyone can go there. Ordinary people like you and me, we need someone like Robin to guide us."

Grandmother drew her eyebrows together in puzzlement. "I saw her dance on a videotape. But I think too much is done in the name of beauty." She was thinking of her own feet.

I chose my words with care because I wanted to protect her secret. "Fashions come and go, but that's a fake kind of beauty. Dancing is something else."

Grandmother gazed at me sadly as if a vast ocean still separated us. "Why do you dance? For beauty?"

I took a long time to think. "No," I finally said, "for myself."

Madame studied Grandmother intently—like a ram preparing to fight for control of the flock. "She should be in class, where I can help her."

I stood, feeling helpless, but Ian still hadn't learned to keep his mouth shut. "We don't have the money," Ian said. The quarrel between Madame and Grandmother had proved more promising than the battles between his own new toys.

"Be quiet, Ian," I scolded him.

"Well, it's true." Ian held up his dinosaurs. "These are the first toys I've had in a long time."

"Why haven't you had money?" Grandmother demanded.

I started gathering up our things. "I think you should ask Mom."

Grandmother, though, had had years of practice interrogating children. She leaned her head forward slightly and regarded me over her glasses. "I'm asking you."

Under her hawklike gaze, I felt small and helpless as a rabbit. "It was expensive bringing you over." I added hastily, "Not that any of us mind. We really wanted to."

Grandmother tilted back her head. "But Edward

owns that fine, fancy house, and Georgie has such a big store.''

It was impossible to look her in the eye any longer. "You should really talk to Mom."

Grandmother, though, was ruthless. "Robin, tell me."

I repeated what Mom had told me. "I think the house took all of Uncle Eddy's money. And the store took all of Uncle Georgie's. Or they would have helped."

"So your parents paid for everything?" Grandmother asked incredulously.

I thought of how angry Mom was going to be. "Mom will skin me alive if she knows you found out. Please don't make a fuss."

Madame placed her hands on my shoulders. "Her parents sacrificed many things—including Robin's lessons."

I could feel my cheeks burning. "It's really all right, *Paw-Paw.*" I wouldn't have said that when I had first met her, but now I had come to love her.

However, my grandmother stamped her canes against the concrete. "No, it's not all right. I see I have some things to straighten out."

Though that didn't necessarily apply to ballet lessons, Madame interpreted Grandmother's words in a positive way. Glancing around, Madame whispered conspiratorially to her chum, "Do you feel like shopping next Sunday? I know of a very good church fair."

Grandmother leaned forward eagerly, and in the same low voice asked, "Good bargains?"

"Those fools don't know true values." Madame dismissed them with a wave of her hand.

Grandmother's eyes lit up at the thought of more prizes. "I would like that," she said.

Madame placed a hand on Grandmother's shoulder. "I would like that too. Nine-thirty next Sunday, then. We want to be there when the doors first open."

Grandmother put a hand on Madame's shoulder in return. "I'll be ready," she assured her.

Grandmother wouldn't discuss the matter any more as we walked home. Now that she had spoken her mind, Madame insisted on escorting us. I got out my key and went up to get money from the emergency fund in the cookie jar. When I returned, I found Madame giving Grandmother a hug and a kiss.

"I will see you very soon," Madame declared grandly—as if it would be a tragedy if she did not.

"Very soon," Grandmother insisted.

Even Ian was impressed enough by Madame to allow her to kiss him. When Madame turned to me, I handed the money to her and asked, "Did you find your Stokowski?"

"Six of them—cheap. No one wants records anymore," she said smugly, and gave me a hug as well.

As Madame went down the steps, Mom appeared at

the top and called down to us, "Where have you been? I've been worried sick." I hadn't seen her when I went into the kitchen, so she must have been in the back.

"We were shopping," Grandmother announced. "Show your mother," she urged me.

I lifted the bag above my head like a trophy. "She got some real bargains too."

"And I got some toys." Ian held up his dinosaurs.

Mom received the news with a frown. "Maybe you shouldn't have done so much."

"I'm fine," Grandmother said as she thumped up the stairs with her canes. "You worry too much."

"I thought I'd left you in sensible hands," Mom said to Grandmother, and then stared at me meaningfully.

Grandmother saw the direction of the look and understood it. "Robin wanted to come home," she said, defending me. "But Ian and I were having too much fun."

I was relieved that she didn't tell Mom she knew about the ballet lessons. I figured I was in enough trouble as it was. When she got to the top of the stairs, she didn't even pause for breath: "I want to use the telephone."

"Are you calling Hong Kong?" I could see Mom making mental calculations about the time difference.

"I might," Grandmother said coyly. "Will the phone reach into the bedroom?"

"Oh, yes," Mom said dryly. "It was in Robin's

room so much it left dents in the floor." She indicated the phone on the little stand in the hallway, "Help *Paw-Paw.*"

We left Ian to show Mom his dinosaurs while I carried Grandmother's purchases and the telephone, unreeling the line behind me. It hadn't occurred to me that she knew how to use the telephone, because she never seemed to use it here. However, we had called her in Hong Kong, so she must have had one there.

Grandmother sat down on her bed with a sigh. "Get the little blue book in the top drawer." She jabbed her cane at the dresser.

I set the phone down beside her, and put her treasures on the floor. When I opened the drawer, I could smell the bars of fragrant sandalwood soap she kept among her clothes to keep them smelling nice. The little blue book was right on top.

"How do I ring up someone in San Francisco?" she asked.

"You just dial the seven-digit number," I said. "Do you want me to help you?"

"No." She switched on the light on the nightstand. "I can manage."

When I saw her tilt back her head and squint through her glasses at a page, I asked her, "Are you sure you don't want me to dial for you?"

She shoved her glasses a little farther down her nose. "Be a good girl and leave your grandmother alone. There's some Chinese I don't want you to learn."

Though I shut the door behind me, I lingered a moment. Inside I could hear her talking in Chinese in a firm tone. Perhaps she had some friends who had moved to San Francisco, and she was bragging to them about her loot in a way that wasn't proper for granddaughters to hear. I thought it was nice that she was finally sinking down roots here. I liked having her around—even if she did like to go to garage sales.

FOURTEEN

The Mermaid

The medical center covered one side of a hill like a bad rash. Mom insisted on coming with me, though I told her she didn't need to. When we went into the waiting room that late afternoon, there were all kinds of people of all ages, from babies to the elderly. And half of them were coughing like they had the plague.

"I think it's more dangerous waiting to see the doctor," I muttered to Mom as we went to the counter.

Mom was too busy checking in with the receptionist to answer. Then we ran a gauntlet of germs to a relatively quiet corner. When my name was finally called, Mom clutched at my wrist. "Did you remember to wash your feet?"

"Mother, puh-lease, why don't you just paint an announcement on the wall," I said. "But if it will make your mind feel any easier, yes I did."

Reassured, Mom sat back in her chair as I went over

to a nurse in green. She led me down a sterile hallway that seemed all linoleum and cinder blocks. Even the light from the panels overhead was harsh.

"The doctor will be with you in a moment," the nurse said with a smile. She indicated an examining table in the middle of the room, but I went over and sat on a chair. Examining tables were for sick people.

I'd barely begun to count the bottles behind a locked cabinet door when Leah's mother, Dr. Brown, breezed in. She was petite like her daughter and had the same earnest smile as Leah. "Hello, Robin. Your parents said you've been having trouble."

"You know how parents are," I said nervously. "They like to worry about everything."

With a sympathetic laugh, she motioned me over toward the scales. After she had noted my weight and measured my height, she consulted the charts in my file. "You've really shot up this last year, haven't you."

"Well, you know how it is," I said.

"Exactly." She patted the examining table. "Hop up here, please."

When I sat down, she motioned for me to take off my shoes. "Let's see your feet."

I stripped off my shoes and socks, and she became very intent. She started poking and prodding and straightening out my toes, asking each time if it hurt.

Sometimes it did, but I lied and said they were fine. Even so, I didn't fool her one minute. With a sigh, she stood up. "You've got hammer toes, young lady."

"Is that bad?" I asked.

"No, it's correctable. It happens when you wear tight shoes. I expect it from some vain middle-aged lady who wears shoes that are too small. Has there been any other strenuous exercise that you've overdone? Have you taken up track at school?"

My feet felt cold as they dangled in the air. "No."

She picked up my shoe and examined the instep, trying to see the size. "Well, these seem fine at least. What have you been doing lately?"

"Nothing, really."

She pulled a pen from her green coat. "Well, this condition couldn't have started at ballet lessons. Madame Oblamov really supervises her students."

I didn't want Madame to get the blame, or worse, be shut down. "No, I've been practicing on my own."

Frowning, Dr. Brown made a notation. "And where have you been practicing?"

"In the living room sometimes, but mostly in the garage," I said.

Dr. Brown looked up sharply. "On a cement floor?" When I nodded, she drew her eyebrows together in concentration. "And what did you wear? Ballet slippers?"

I squirmed. "No, Madame said I was ready for toe shoes."

Dr. Brown scribbled something else in my folder. "And when did you buy a pair last?"

"A while ago," I said.

She barked out the questions like a prosecutor. "How long? Six months? A year?"

"Over a year," I said softly, already knowing what was to blame.

"This problem usually takes several years," she said. "And even then, at your age, it should only create a predisposition to that condition."

"I'm a quick learner." I shrugged.

"Do you have your toe shoes with you?" she demanded. When I shook my head, she made another note. "I'd like to see them, but I suspect that's the problem—that and the concrete floor."

I seized on the only real hope now. "You said the hammer toes were correctable."

"There's an operation," Dr. Brown said. "But you might not be able to dance again."

I felt a huge lump catch in my throat. "And if I don't . . ."

Dr. Brown closed the file and cleared her throat. "Well, we can keep it from getting worse, but it will hurt when you dance."

"I don't care," I pleaded. "I just want to dance."

"I think that's something to discuss with your parents." Slipping her pen into her pocket, she turned her back toward me. There was something in the way she did it that told me there would be no appeal.

When she went out, I put on my socks and shoes again. I had just finished tying the laces when Dr. Brown returned with Mom. "I don't think she understands the full implications," she said.

"You don't know Robin." Mom sighed.

On purpose, I went up on pointe to show her that I was fine. "I don't want any operations if it means I can't dance."

"You really sprouted this year. I never thought about your ballet shoes," Mom said guiltily.

"You bought me regular shoes for school." I shrugged, trying to give her a way out.

However, Mom immediately turned the blame on me: "Why didn't you tell us your ballet shoes were too tight?" she demanded sternly.

I tried my best to defend myself: "Because you would have told me to stop dancing rather than buy me new ones."

Mom knew that was true. "Robin, there's more to life than dancing."

I thought of that moment in front of the footlights. "Not for me," I said stubbornly.

There was a spark in Mom's eyes. I knew she would use my feet as an excuse not to spend the money on lessons. "Your health comes first."

I knew I had to provide alternatives or I was heading straight for surgery. And then Mom would use the medical costs as an excuse to keep me from dancing. "Doctor, can you operate on me later?"

Dr. Brown inclined her head slightly. "Yes, but I don't recommend it."

"And in the meantime you said that you could keep it from getting worse," I reminded her.

Again she dipped her head reluctantly. "Well, yes, but Robin, you'll be in some pain."

"Dancers get aches and pains." I shrugged.

"You see what I'm up against?" Mom appealed to the doctor.

"Leah would be just as stubborn." Dr. Brown sighed. "So talk it over with your husband." And they held an urgent, whispered conversation until I got close to them.

"I know you have my number, but here it is anyway so you can have it handy. Call me anytime." Dr. Brown held out a card to Mom as I drew near. "I'll be happy to come over and explain everything to Gil."

Mom took the card thoughtfully. "I will."

As we headed back outside, I tried to work on Mom: "I've been waiting for almost a year to begin lessons again. Everyone's so much further ahead."

Mom, though, was glad to have a medical reason not to spend money on ballet lessons. "You're not thinking things through, Robin." Mom clutched the doctor's card in her hand. "Part of growing up is learning to live within your limits."

I could see my ballet lessons floating away, so I snatched the card from her hand. "What's the use of being good all the time then?" I could feel tears stinging my eyes. I wished the card was that stupid doctor as I tore it up into a dozen bits.

As nurses began to poke their heads out of rooms, Mom pressed her lips together into a thin line. She didn't believe in public spectacles. "We'll discuss this later."

It was funny, but as soon as we got home, we both sought out Grandmother to recruit her as an ally. She was in the living room coloring a book with Ian. "What did the doctor say?" she asked, and then saw our faces. "Is it bad news?"

"Ian, we have to discuss something. Why don't you watch a little television." Mom rummaged around in the cabinet beneath the TV.

"What did the doctor say?" Ian echoed Grandmother as he looked up from his book.

Mom popped *Wolf Warriors* into the VCR. "It's adult stuff."

"Robin isn't an adult," Ian said stubbornly. "She's just a kid, like me." But his head swiveled to watch the cartoon.

"Right now, she is definitely being childish," Mom said.

"Let's talk in the kitchen." Grandmother put down her crayon and reached for her canes.

We helped her rise from the rug and head for the kitchen. Once there, she sank onto a kitchen chair while Mom put water in a kettle for tea.

* * *

"So," she said once Mom had explained, "if Robin does have the operation, she will be free from pain, but she may not be able to dance. But if she does not have the operation, she will have some pain, but she will be able to dance."

"But they can keep it from getting worse," I pointed out.

Grandmother started to shake her head. "I don't think you should."

"You see," Mom said triumphantly, as if that ended the matter of my lessons once and for all.

"But Mom says you feel a lot worse pain," I said, trying to get Grandmother to side with me.

"It's just like they said about the Little Mermaid. It's like walking on knives," she conceded.

"Well, this won't be anything like that." I looked around the table. "Athletes and other dancers have to go through injuries all the time."

"You don't understand the cost of living all the time with that kind of pain everyday." Grandmother took my hand.

I squeezed her hand tightly. "But it's not because of some stupid prejudices. It's because I love it. You must have danced in China. Or run. Or jumped."

She thought for a moment and then sighed. "That's so long ago I don't remember."

Or didn't want to, I thought. "Didn't you ever love

something so much that it hurt?" I pressed my free hand against my chest.

"I loved my children that way," she said. I could hear the ache in her voice. "But I gave them up because I knew it was for the best."

On the burner the kettle began to dance, rattling on the iron grate. As Mom got up to turn it off, she said, "And we know what's best for you, Robin."

I pulled at Grandmother's arm to get back her attention. I felt like I was fighting for my life. "What did your mother say to you when she told you she was going to bind your feet?"

Grandmother had a faraway look in her eyes as she started to recall those old days. "I didn't want to lose my feet. But my mother insisted."

I hurt for her. "How awful."

"This is totally different," Mom argued, and tried to distract herself by getting out cups. "I'm trying to keep you from getting crippled."

"The doctor said they could keep it from getting worse," I said, and then gripped Grandmother's hand desperately. *"Paw-Paw,* if you were good at something, wouldn't you want to do it?"

She sandwiched my hand between both of hers. "You're so young. You have so much life."

"When I dance, I feel so . . ." I hunted for the right word and remembered how it was on the night of the recital, "so . . . free. Like I could fly forever."

She tilted back her head with sudden comprehension. "I saw it on your face when we watched the videotape."

I leaned forward urgently. "Don't let them steal that freedom away from me like they stole it from you."

Grandmother lifted away a hand to stroke her chin. "You said dancing won't make your feet worse?"

"Not as long as I can have new shoes," I assured her.

She stared at me sharply. "What is wrong with your old ones?"

"They . . ." I hesitated when I saw Mom. She was shaking her head.

"Tell me what's wrong," Grandmother insisted in annoyance. When I remained silent, she turned to Mom. "I order you to tell me what's wrong."

Mom's shoulders rose and fell in a large sigh. "They're too small."

"Then why didn't you buy new shoes?" Grandmother asked. Suddenly she sat back as she understood. "Because you were trying to bring me over." She turned to Mom. "You should have left me in Hong Kong rather than have this happen."

"It's done," Mom said, pouring the hot water into the cups. "Let's not blame ourselves."

I hated to see Grandmother's horrified expression. "I'd rather have you than anything."

Grandmother gripped my hand with renewed energy. "I never meant to hurt you."

"I know that." I pleaded silently with my eyes: *Let me dance.*

Grandmother tilted back her head. "You could always have the operation later?"

"Yes." I didn't think that day would ever come, though. "Let me dance."

Grandmother looked thoughtful. "You choose to walk on knives. For what you love—like the Little Mermaid."

Even if the pain had been as great as hers, I would have done it. "Yes," I said.

Grandmother reached her free hand out toward Mom. "Let her."

Mom slammed the box of tea bags down. "I can't." When she turned around, I could see that she was almost in tears herself. "So don't ask me."

Grandmother's hand groped through the air toward Mom. "She's not your baby anymore. She's old enough to make her own decision on this."

Mom looked at me as if she could feel every painful step herself. "You don't know what you're asking."

"But I do," Grandmother said. "I let you go when I wanted to keep you." Leaning forward, she grasped Mom's hand. "Let her go now."

Mom let herself be pulled back toward the table. "Gil will never go along with it."

"Yes, he will." Grandmother drew her fist in so that it touched mine. "I have got eyes and ears. He has always wanted what Robin wants. He took her side on the lessons, didn't he?"

"Well, yes," Mom admitted reluctantly.

"You are the one who has to let Robin try. If things get worse, she'll accept the operation." She glanced at me and I nodded. But I had faith that day would never come. But would Mom obey her own mother on the ballet lessons?

Mom covered her face with her free hand. "We'll talk about it later, Robin. All right?"

I knew the issue had shifted back to money again. I was positive that when we talked later she would postpone my lessons for financial reasons. However, for the sake of peace, I swallowed. "Okay."

FIFTEEN

The Dinner

The rest of the day, though, Mom found excuses to avoid being alone with me. I didn't mind at all. I figured she was just going to use our poverty as an excuse not to let me dance.

We were all surprised that evening when the doorbell rang and Uncle Georgie and Uncle Eddy came in. "Mom," I called up the stairs, "it's your favorite brothers."

Mom leaned over the banister, adjusting her hair. When she saw it was indeed her brothers, she demanded, "Why didn't you warn me? I don't have anything ready."

"We can go pick up some stuff," Uncle Georgie said as he began to climb the stairs. He was wearing a satin Porsche jacket. Uncle Eddy was in a suit, but his tie was loosened. Under his arm, he had a package.

I made a note to myself to tie Dad to a chair. This time Uncle Georgie could go to some place that took credit cards—or learn how to wash dishes.

Dad came into the hallway to greet them. "Georgie, Eddy, what are you doing here?"

"Can't a fellow miss his mother?" Georgie asked.

As we passed Dad, I hooked my arm through his. "Let Uncle Georgie go alone this time," I whispered.

"We can afford it," Dad said, as if it was a point of honor.

"No, we can't," Mom, who had overheard us, said. "Let the big shot go get dinner."

While Uncle Eddy and Uncle Georgie headed to the living room, I went to Grandmother's door and knocked. "*Paw-Paw*, you have visitors."

Her voice came through the door: "Really? Who is it?"

"Your sons," I said.

"What a surprise," she said, but when she opened her door, I saw that she was already dressed up in her best and had put on makeup.

As I trailed her into the living room, I began to suspect that something was up, but I couldn't figure out what.

When she entered the living room, Uncle Georgie got up and hugged her. "Sorry we didn't call ahead."

"I like surprises," she said, and gave Eddy a hug. "Did you know that Robin is a dancer?"

"You couldn't miss it," Uncle Georgie said as he helped her sit down.

And if it was such a big surprise, why did Uncle Eddy hand her the package without a word of explanation—as if Grandmother had expected it?

Cradling the package on her lap, she ordered me, "Put on the tape with you dancing."

I glanced at Mom, who had forbidden us to play it again, but she just shrugged. "If *Paw-Paw* wants to see it, go ahead."

I thought of all the beginners' flubs, and I nodded to Uncle Georgie and Uncle Eddy. "They don't want to see it."

"You're very good. Don't be modest," Grandmother ordered.

As Ian played with his toys and made dinosaur noises, I put the tape into the machine. "Do you want me to fast-forward to my part?"

"Yes," Uncle Georgie and Eddy both said.

"No," Grandmother said at the same time, and since Grandmother's vote counted ten times more than any other single vote, she won.

Afraid that I would cry again, I joined Ian in his games—even though the sole function of my dinosaur was to provide the main course for his Tyrannosaurus Rex.

When the tape was finally over, Uncle Georgie said, "Great." I didn't know whether he meant the dancing or was referring to the fact that it was now over.

Grandmother looked from one son to the other. "Robin has a great talent."

"She sure does," Uncle Georgie said, and Uncle Eddy nodded meekly.

"So the entire family would agree that it would be a shame to waste such promise," Grandmother added. And to my surprise, their heads bobbed up and down once more.

As I rewound the tape, Mom asked, "Well, where should I call for food?"

"Even when Georgie was a boy, he always knew the best places in Hong Kong," Grandmother said quickly. "I bet it's the same here. You go someplace, Georgie."

Uncle Georgie got up promptly. "Yes, Mother."

I wondered if Grandmother had heard us grumbling about the last time. I was beginning to think that she didn't miss much.

"And next time you and Eddy don't come empty-handed," Grandmother scolded him. "I like seeing you, but you should bring cookies or candy or toys for the little ones. I taught you better manners than that."

"Yes, Mother," Eddy said.

"You want to come along, Gil?" Uncle Georgie asked Dad.

Mom quickly grabbed him. "You've got to help me set the table."

"Henpecked, huh?" Uncle Georgie asked.

"I got him trained," Mom said, refusing to let go of Dad.

Dad squirmed, but Mom would not release him until we heard the door slam behind Uncle Georgie.

Uncle Eddy turned to Grandmother then: "You know, Mother, Marilyn decided that our bedroom was too hot. All that sun, you know. So we're going to move into the front room. If you don't mind the master bedroom, you're welcome to it."

"I would like that fine," Grandmother said before any of us could react.

"Are you sure, Mother?" Mom asked in surprise.

"You have been very generous, but it's time," Grandmother said. "The little ones need more room."

"But I don't mind," I blurted out.

"You're growing up." Grandmother smiled. "This is a time when you especially need your privacy."

Even though I would have welcomed the announcement at any time in the last few weeks, now that we had become closer, I didn't want her to leave—even if it meant sleeping on the floor. Ian was already bawling, and I felt like doing the same thing myself. "Why don't you think about it?" I urged.

"Don't be selfish," Uncle Eddy scolded me. "You have to share your grandmother."

"You come visit me," Grandmother said.

Uncle Eddy tapped his fingers on the arm of the sofa. "We're only a ten-minute bus ride away on the other side of the park."

◆ ◆ ◆

We worked out the details of the move—Grandmother would leave us in only two weeks—and then Uncle Eddy caught us up on the rest of his family's doings.

When Uncle Georgie returned with a feast, I helped Mom and Dad pour the cartons into the shallow, wide bowls. "Is it possible that Georgie and Eddy are finally growing up?" Dad asked.

Mom defended her little brothers. "They were always grown up."

"Not while they had you taking care of everything," Dad said. "Even when they were first married, they still brought their shirts to you to sew their buttons on."

"Their wives were more specialized." Mom patted Dad's cheek. "You don't realize how lucky you are, Gil."

"And now they have Grandmother . . ." I pointed out.

"Amen to that," Dad muttered. At Mom's dark look, he added hastily, "Just kidding."

When we sat down at the dinner table, everyone could see that Uncle Georgie hadn't stinted on food. "What'd you do? Sign a government contract?" Uncle Eddy teased his brother.

"I know the head cook at this place," Uncle Georgie said. "He used to pack 'em into Chinatown. Now that he's got a place in Richmond, people even leave Chinatown to eat out here." He held up a bowl to pass to Grandmother. "And for you, Mother, he made . . ." He said something in Chinese.

When I glanced at Mom, she translated: "Soy sauce squab."

Uncle Eddy chuckled. "Georgie, remember when we first came here and you saw all the pigeons in Union Square?"

"Yeah, yeah, that's ancient history," Uncle Georgie said as he handed the dish to Grandmother.

Uncle Eddy still reminded him: "You tried to set up a trap to catch and sell them."

Mom held up a napkin to her mouth as she laughed. "I had to work overtime to pay the fines."

They began to reminisce with Grandmother about their days in Hong Kong. Because Grandmother was usually working, they had grown up half in the streets there. "I bet you think your mother is real prim and proper, don't you, Robin?" Uncle Georgie asked.

"Isn't she?" I asked.

Mom stiffened in her chair. "I don't think the children need to hear about that."

However, Uncle Georgie was happy to humiliate someone else for a change with his memories. "Hey, Eddy, remember the time that kung-fu hotshot challenged anyone to knock him out of his stance?"

"Stance?" Ian asked.

Uncle Eddy shoved his chair back and stood up. "It

was the horse stance." He crouched slightly with knees bent, as if he were riding a horse.

Uncle George shoved at the air. "And nobody could knock him over, though we all tried. Even Eddy and me both together."

Mom pretended to focus on a piece of duck on her plate. "He shouldn't have made fun of you. He was crude."

Uncle Eddy sat back down. "So your mom comes up, and the hotshot gets ready." Uncle Eddy stuck out his chest and held his fists near his waist. "And he tells your mom to shove as hard as she can."

Uncle Georgie was already slapping the table as he laughed. "So she shoves and shoves. And the hotshot starts to tease her."

Mom frowned. "He was even cruder to me."

"So she rears back, and *koosh*." Uncle Eddy punched at the air. "Right in the jaw. Sent him flying."

Mom squirmed uncomfortably in her chair. "He deserved it."

"Yeah, but then he took it out on us for a whole year," Uncle Georgie said. "I had his footprint stamped into my backside."

Dad was laughing nearly as hard as our uncles. He glanced at Mom affectionately—so maybe the angry murmurings from their bedroom would end. "Did you know you had such a wildcat?" he asked Grandmother.

"I heard," Grandmother said. "That's when I de-cided to send her to America."

As the laughter subsided, Mom turned to her mother. "You never told me."

"You didn't need to know," Grandmother said, and nodded first to Uncle Georgie and Uncle Eddy. "And that's why I sent these two as soon as I could." And I could see the sadness in her eyes at having lost her children all those years.

"You should have come over sooner," I said to her.

"I knew I was going to be a burden as soon as I got here," Grandmother said. "I wanted my children to establish themselves."

And I found myself marveling at her strength and self-sacrifice. I could see how she had crossed the country on her crippled feet with her three children. I was just glad that she was in my corner now.

"You know, you're going to make Robin think we were punks back there." Uncle Georgie toyed with a piece of beef. "Our friends in Hong Kong wound up real big shots."

"And some of them wound up dead," Grand-mother said.

"The streets are just as mean in San Francisco as in Hong Kong," Uncle Eddy said.

Dad tried to play the peacemaker. "Well, you're all over here, and everyone's a success story."

"But I've noticed one thing." Grandmother pre-tended to frown at Mom. "In America children are too idle. They need something to occupy more of their time," she announced. "For instance, Robin should take dancing lessons."

"Of course," Mom said, but she looked at me warningly so I knew better than to count on it.

Grandmother glanced at Uncle George and then at Uncle Eddy and gave a nod.

"I've been meaning to give you this, sis." Uncle Georgie took out a red *li-see* from his shirt pocket. It was a small rectangle with gold decorations on it.

Uncle Eddy slipped one from his suit pocket. "Sorry we're late," he said. "You know how things are."

Mom took Uncle Eddy's and put it away to look at later. She had once told me that was the Chinese way to do it. However, Dad was closer to Uncle Georgie so he accepted the *li-see* for Mom.

Though Dad was sensitive about many Chinese customs, it didn't apply to presents. He'd open his Christmas presents whenever he could find where we had hidden them. So he naturally couldn't resist opening the envelope and pulling out the check.

"We'll do that later, Gil," Mom whispered.

However, it was already too late. Dad had opened Uncle Georgie's check. Though he didn't say anything, his eyes widened and he passed it on to Mom. When she saw it, her eyebrows twitched. "Georgie, are you sure?"

"Yeah, sure, sis." Uncle Georgie grinned. He

glanced at Grandmother and received her approving nod. I was sure one of her calls had gone to him.

"You've done a lot for us, sis," Uncle Eddy said. "It's only fair." I was sure his check would equal Uncle Georgie's.

Mom was so overwhelmed that she got up and went around the table to give each of them a kiss. And she gave the biggest to Dad. Of course, once she sat down she was fair game again for embarrassing memories of Hong Kong.

Afterward, when they had left and I was alone with Grandmother and Mom, I made a point of going over to Grandmother, where she sat alone in her chair. "How did you do it?" I whispered.

"I reminded them that they should make as many sacrifices as their sister has. And," she brought one eyelid down in an elaborate wink, "I also threatened to move in with them."

"But you *are* moving in with Uncle Eddy," I said.

"Only long enough for him to make an apartment for me down in the garage. He calls it an in-law apartment." She enunciated the syllables carefully, as if she had just learned them that day.

"But I don't want you to go," I said, putting my arm around her.

She patted my shoulder. "I can see how crowded you are. A growing girl needs room to grow."

"You've got to visit us lots," I said.

"And you visit me," she said.

"With cookies." I laughed.

"With plenty of cookies," she said firmly, and then opened the paper bag Uncle Eddy had given her. "No one's going to think my grandchild is a beggar who has to wear old shoes."

Dumbfounded, I just stared. "But how did you know my size?"

"I peeked at your regular shoes. You said your old shoes needed ribbons. I suppose these do too?" She prodded me with the toes until I took them.

Mom came over and took the bag from her. "I'll sew the ribbons on."

"No," Grandmother said. "Show me, and I'll do it."

Mom got her sewing kit from the closet. From it, she lifted the ribbons from my old shoes and draped them across the arm of Grandmother's chair. "Would you like me to thread the needle for you?"

"Yes." Grandmother held up her hands for the shoes. "Where do the ribbons go, Robin?"

I showed her the spots, but when I saw her squinting, I added, "You don't have to though."

"I want to."

We waited as Mom held the needle up toward the light and slipped the thread through the eye. Then she tied off the thread and broke the connection to the spool.

Grandmother took the threaded needle and began to work. I marveled at the skill that sent the needle slipping back and forth with a steadiness that spoke of long years of practice.

As she sewed, I saw that her wrist was small—just like mine. And just like Mother's. And branching over the skin of their wrists I saw the same delicate pattern of veins like blue-green ribbons. And through those ribbons I knew the same blood pulsed and the same hearts beat. Ribbons of life. Ribbons that bound us together forever.

When she was done, she held them out to me triumphantly. "You will be my legs. When you dance, I will dance."

I slipped my feet into the cool cloth and tied the ribbons. Then I sprang to my feet to hug her. "Thank you for giving dancing back to me."

"You just be happy," she said, returning my hug just as fiercely.

I was so delighted in fact that I began to cry, and of course that set off Mom and Grandmother.

When Ian drifted into the room, he regarded me suspiciously. "What did you do now, Robin? Why is everyone crying?"

I loved Ian so much right at that moment that I could have gobbled him down whole. Instead, I settled on pulling him against me tightly. "Because we love one another."

"You're getting me wet." Ian squirmed away indignantly.

"I'll get you wetter," Grandmother said, and pressed her cheek against his as she started to tickle him.

In no time, Ian had dissolved into a fit of giggles, lying as helplessly at Grandmother's feet as a boneless pink lump. "Help," he shrieked between giggles.

So I joined in tickling him.

"Help *me*, not *Paw-Paw*," he yelled.

"I can't hear you over the giggling," I said, continuing to tickle him with Grandmother.

Mom wiped her eyes hastily with the back of one hand. "Careful," she warned, "or he'll get the—"

Ian twitched as he gave a monstrous hiccup.

"Now see what you've done," he said accusingly as he sat up.

As he gave another hiccup, I stretched out my hands like claws. "We'll just have to scare them out of you."

He tried to run, but Grandmother caught him. "No fair," he said, wriggling in her arms.

"You asked for it," I said, and began to tickle him again so that the giggles replaced the hiccups once more.

· A F T E R W O R D ·

As a practice, footbinding is believed to have begun in the tenth century A.D. Whatever its true origins, footbinding did not become a popular custom until after the fourteenth century. In 1911, when China became an American-style Republic, the practice was officially outlawed.

Unofficially, however, some girls in rural areas had their feet bound until 1949, when the Communists took over. As late as 1983, there were an estimated two million women with bound feet who still lived in China. Because many of the women chose to keep their feet bound rather than live in constant pain, an estimated million special shoes were made for them each year at a children's shoe factory in China.

See Priscilla Wegars, "Besides Polly Bemis" in *Hidden Heritage.*
"Crippling Legacy of Bound Feet" in San Francisco *Chronicle,* July 27, 1990.
"The Golden Lotus Stigma." Associated Press, 1987.

FIC   Yep, Laurence.
YEP   Ribbons.

20349

$15.95

DATE		
OC24 '96		
OC28 '96		
NO25 '96		
96 DE9 630 '96		
MA27 '98		
00 7 '99 29 '99		
OC28 '99		
N 5 '00		

D0101627